Skin Deep

by

Bill Clem

PublishAmerica
Baltimore

ISBN: 1-4241-3173-1
PUBLISHED BY PUBLISHAMERICA, LLLP
www.publishamerica.com
Baltimore

Printed in the United States of America

For my wife and children. Thanks for all the love and support. And for Shi Shi, for hanging out at the computer for all those lonely hours.

I would like to thank the folks at PublishAmerica for giving me the opportunity to release this book. Also, I would be amiss if I didn't thank Gary Wilkinson for being an astute reader of my work, early on. And special thanks to my wife, Susan, for giving me input on the ending.

Prologue

The fire started quietly on that Friday night in August when his life changed forever.

At 2:00 A.M., twelve-year-old David Reel, sat up in bed with such suddenness that he felt overwhelmed with a sense of fear. He had no idea what had awakened him, but guessed it was some noise or movement.

Had something touched him?

He stayed still, holding his breath, and stared straight ahead, listening. At first he was disoriented, but as his mind took in his limited field of vision, he remembered he was in his own room. At about the same instant that he realized where he was, David perceived it was the middle of the night. *And he smelled smoke!*

David, and his best friend, Sam, were having their weekly get together, and it was Sam's turn to be the guest.

Sam and his younger sister, Molly, lived across the street with their aunt Lyla. She had taken them after an auto accident, which killed their parents, spared the two children. Lyla was as good a mother as any child could ask for.

David's mother raised him alone. Ten years earlier, they'd reported his father lost in action in Hanoi. The boys felt a common bond since they both lacked a father, and in Sam's case, a mother as well. Despite this, he and Sam remained optimistic, always dreaming that they would both have a new father some day.

Now, as he awoke in the middle of the night, the house that always evoked hope and reassurance for David, suddenly seemed like an ominous place. David felt himself inexplicitly paralyzed by a sensation of acute terror. His mouth was dry. He attributed this to fear, as he continued to lie perfectly still like a wary animal, his senses straining for any disturbance.

David had often felt the same way after awakening in the night from a bad dream. If he didn't move, perhaps the monsters would go away.

The smell of smoke began to overwhelm him.

David felt his terror become panic. Now he was certain something terrible was happening. He had to get help.

He couldn't see much of the room, especially since the only illumination came from a small floor-level night-light behind his bed. All he could see was the indistinct juncture of ceiling and wall. Silhouetted against it was the shadow of his baseball bat and glove.

Yanking his head off the pillow, David bounded onto the floor and instantly felt the heat beneath him. With the door closed, smoke streamed under it and began to surround him. Sam was asleep on the other side. David ran to him and grabbed him by the shoulders. "Sam, get up."

Sam's eyes opened. They quickly widened when he saw the smoke. "What's happening?" he screamed.

"The house is on fire. We have to get out of here!"

"Out the window," Sam said. He leaped out of bed and pushed the lower window up.

David looked out the window. Flames rushed up the side of the house with lethal purpose. "We can't get out that way."

Running to the door, noxious fumes choked him as the carpet began to melt under his feet. He managed to grab his shoes and get on the bed just as the molten carpet burst into flames. The smoke was now as thick as stone and a low rumble got louder every second. It was as if the Gates of Hell had opened up and swallowed the house.

David crouched down by the door and heard his mother scream.

"Mom." His voice surprised him with its weakness. He'd intended to yell, but only a hoarse whisper came out. At the same time, his head felt tremendously heavy, requiring all his strength to keep it upright.

He looked back for Sam, but his room was a solid gray curtain. David grabbed the door knob, then instantly pulled back his hand in a rush of pain. The seared flesh sizzled.

"Mom," he screamed.

Somehow he organized his thoughts enough to find a shirt. He covered the knob and tried to turn it. Finally, with horrendous effort, he yanked it open and staggered out the door. He tottered a few steps and went down to his knees, choking, coughing hard, wheezing with panic. He crawled toward the stairs. The heat was suffocating and David felt a new surge of fright: *he would burn alive before he could get out.*

"Sam," he yelled. David felt certain he was dead. The heat exacerbated the pain in his already scorched hands and his knees burnt from the carpet that had now turned to lava.

Panic and desperation filled David's consciousness, but he tried to focus his thoughts. He had to get to his mother. There was a ringing in his ears, a sense of revolving, nausea.

Then blackness...

* * *

Charlie Goodman could see an inferno had already fully engulfed the Reel residence by the time his fire company arrived. The flames so hot they threatened neighboring houses. They went to work with the hoses and got the fire under control enough to send in men to look for survivors. *No one expected any.*

The gruesome remains of the first body were burned beyond recognition. It was a small body and would take dental records to identify it. The second victim, a woman, and perhaps the most tragic of all, was barely alive. Her hair was burned away, and her face was like some skinned animal. It was a sin she had survived.

When Charlie Goodman found the boy in the back yard, he was in such a state of shock that at first he could not speak and was too dazed to even cry.

"My mother...Sam? Where are my mother and Sam?" he begged in a stricken voice that would haunt Charlie for years. "I couldn't save my mother."

Fire engines and emergency vehicles choked the narrow street, red lights revolving, ambulance radios crackling with excited voices.

When the final piece of roof collapsed, a cry of dismay arose from stunned neighbors, gathered in a knot across the street. Unable to believe Hell, had landed on Gilbert Road. Final masses of dark smoke billowed above them, then floated westward like a dark shroud.

* * *

One lady held a small child and stood back from the crowd. She didn't want the child to see it. She herself was in a state of shock.

Sam's aunt Lyla, and his five-year-old sister, Molly.

Chapter One

Twenty Years Later

Dr. David Reel's BMW sedan rolled to a stop in front of the Twinbrook Industrial Center. The parking lot sat nearly deserted, a patchwork of shadows and evenly spaced pools of light from the halogen street-lamps. Inside sat David Reel's lab.

Sighing, he paused a moment to think about his week. Despite the pride the lab evoked, he realized he had some mixed feelings about his success. In his heart David was a surgeon, yet driven by the memory of his mother and the suffering she had endured, he had become more of a scientist and less doctor. Even his patients had noticed; his office time had become increasingly scarce.

Growing skin from discarded fetal tissue was an idea David had conceived while still a pre med. student at the University of Maryland. His minor in biochemistry provided him the background he needed to test out his hypothesis while still pursuing his dream of becoming a plastic surgeon. David spent countless hours in the school lab while his roommates pursued more typical collegiate pastimes. He was happy to sacrifice his social life in the name of science. He knew there had to be a better way to do skin grafts, and if he could find it, no one would have to suffer as his mother did.

Now, at age thirty-two, after many years of postgraduate biomedical research, some of it involving live animals, he had finally succeeded. With a mixture of apprehension and curiosity, he had invited Paul Gallo to his lab tonight. He was ready to unveil it to the public, but he wanted to see the reaction of an individual first. And David knew Paul would appreciate what he was about to show him.

What plastic surgeon wouldn't? Also, David could trust him. That was of *paramount* importance.

Nonetheless, David felt anxious. To his surprise he did not experience the same sense of triumph he'd enjoyed during his initial discovery when he had marveled at the power of science and his own creativity. Instead of jubilation David felt a sense of growing unease. It had started a week earlier while contemplating the final phase of his work. The effect was the same every time he thought about it: perspiration appeared on his forehead and his heart raced. He had to inhale deeply to calm himself.

The sudden appearance of headlights in his rear view mirror jarred David out of his depressing reverie.

Paul Gallo pulled in next to him and stepped out. He was a short stocky Italian who combed his thin hair like Julius Ceaser. He still wore his hospital surgical scrubs. Even the paper mask dangled around his neck.

Though Paul had become an indubitably faithful friend, it had not started out that way. When David first opened his practice, Paul was already a well-respected plastic surgeon in Washington. He considered David a competitor, although David always felt there were plenty of breast implants and rhinoplasties to go around. As David started to dedicate more time to research, however, Paul turned out to be indispensable. He had handled many referrals, giving David more time to spend in the lab. He often told Paul if it wasn't for his help, his success would have taken longer.

David stepped out and grasped Paul's outstretched hand.

They greeted each other enthusiastically.

"Glad you could make it, Paul."

Chapter Two

The fluorescent lights blinked, then filled the room with their rude light. David stepped aside and let Paul Gallo precede him into the lab.

Although Paul had been there on a few occasions, it had always been during the day. It amazed him how sinister the place looked at night with no people to relieve its sterile appearance. That aside, the room was just as impressive as Paul remembered.

The main room was thirty-feet-long and equally wide. Down the middle a row of large glass cylinders stood filled with a pink liquid. Half-inch clear tubing ran from each cylinder to a bank of stainless steel incubators. Several mainframe computers hummed in front of the incubators. Paul marveled at the equipment as he followed David.

Beyond that room and through a glass door was the animal room, where Paul could see rats and mice scurrying around in their cages. Just beside them in a large cage, a baboon paced back and forth.

"That must be the famous, Dexter," Paul said.

"That's him. The star of the show."

Paul watched the ape for a minute.

"This way," David said, guiding him toward to the back wall.

David stopped in front of a huge stainless steel refrigerator and rolled up his right shirt sleeve. "Paul, look at my arm and tell me what you see."

Paul didn't know where this was going, but he went along. "I see a normal size right forearm with perhaps a little too much hair."

David smiled. "Look closer, Paul."

"David, what's this all—"

"Please, indulge me."

"Okay, I've looked closer and I still see the same thing. Your arm."

"Precisely. A normal arm with no marks or scars. Would you agree?"

"Yes, of course."

"What would you say if I told you three weeks ago, I cut a four-inch square out of my forearm, a half inch deep?"

"I'd say, where's the scar to prove it?"

David leaned over the lab table beside him and removed a small envelope. He pulled out several Polaroids and handed them to Paul.

"Does that look like my arm in that first photo? You're a trained plastic surgeon, what do you think?"

"Yes, I'd say that definitely is your arm."

"And this one?"

Paul winced when he saw the next picture. It was indeed, David's arm, but with a large chunk cut out of it. Even for a plastic surgeon, the picture was so close up it was hard to stomach. "It also looks like your arm…minus a piece."

Paul saw what David was getting at. "Are you telling me you repaired your own arm with this lab grown skin?"

"I did, Paul. And as you can see, it's impossible to tell."

"But how? This is incredible. I mean…I expected something good, but this…this is unbelievable!"

David began to pace. His face took on an excited expression, and Paul began to feel slightly uncomfortable.

"I became interested in various proteins and how they reacted with certain enzymes in the body. It was not a new idea. Many had already tested the theory, but no one had found a way to make skin reproduce at the molecular level. I knew if I could find a way to actually tweak a single skin cell into accelerated growth, I would be able to produce laboratory skin on any scale imaginable. You follow me?"

David stopped his pacing to look directly at Paul.

"Yes," Paul said, watching his friend. He seemed to be changing in front of his eyes.

David resumed his pacing as his excitement grew. "I found I could take discarded fetal tissue, usually placental, extract a few cells, then adding an enzyme I discovered in bone matrix, called Sr-23, I was able to grow skin in a petri dish at a rate of one square-inch every twelve hours. By increasing the amount of the enzyme, I can speed up the process even more."

He stopped again in front of Paul. His eyes sparkled. He reached into the refrigerator and slid out a drawer from one of the shelves.

"This is the result."

Paul's jaw dropped open. *Perfect skin!* It was 12 inches square and looked just like newborn skin.

"It's perfect," Paul said, eying it as if it were a jewel.

"Better than perfect. It doesn't scar. You saw for yourself." David held up his arm in front of Paul to drive home the point.

"Tell me, David, what is this matrix made out of?"

"I can't tell you that, Paul. Surely you understand what could happen if—"

"I understand." Paul looked at the back of the lab and noticed the large double doors with OFF LIMITS painted on them in bright red letters.

He looked back at David. *And saw his eyes flash!*

13

Chapter Three

Rufus Davis stood alone on the thick carpet of his boss's office. He could hear his pulse thump beneath his Oriole's ball cap. Over his pulse he heard the voices of patients, muffled by the thick mahogany door.

Shepard Pratt Hospital for the Criminally Insane was one of the most secure mental health institutions on the East Coast, if not the entire United States. They'd never had an escape since they opened their doors in 1949.

Until now.

In the next room, Davis heard a door close and then footsteps filing into the hall. And there was his nemesis coming into the room. Kay Allworth, with her short neck and her butch haircut that spiked up like the quills of a porcupine.

She glared at the huge black orderly.

"Do you realize what you have done?"

Davis looked straight ahead. His arms hung like two country hams at his sides.

Given the hospital's proximity to several prestigious private schools in Baltimore, and the potential threat the escape posed to the students at those schools, Allworth panicked. She blamed security, who blamed the nurses, who in turn blamed the orderlies–who usually–got blamed for everything.

"The girl was here, ma'am. Not ten minutes ago."

"Well obviously she is not now." Her voice began to rise.

While Allworth chastised Davis, the patient, a young woman of twenty-six, calmly got on a Greyhound bus and headed out of Baltimore. Davis would never tell. *He had promised her.* And he didn't like Allworth.

The hospital would keep it quiet as long as possible, lest they panic the community. After all, they could later claim, the staff psychologist proclaimed the girl cured–that is–as long as she took her medication. Unfortunately, it was all left behind at Shepard Pratt. That, of course, would also be kept quiet. Davis would watch it all unfold. Allworth ordered him not to say a word.

By the time the hospital notified the authorities and fabricated their documents to avoid as much scrutiny as possible, nearly five-hours had passed. The public meanwhile, was unaware, that the perpetrator of one of the most deadly acts of arson ever committed— was loose.

Chapter Four

David Reel looked out from beside the podium into the cavernous conference hall of the Sheraton Hotel, Bethesda, Maryland. The Symposium on Plastic Surgery had drawn a standing-room-only crowd.

David, however, was the star of the show. The whole medical establishment, it seemed, anticipated his long awaited announcement. The FDA was about to approve preliminary trials of his new product, aptly called: Reel Skin.

"Our next speaker is David Reel, M.D.," the conference monitor intoned. "His discussion is entitled, 'The Future of Skin Grafting.'" David stepped up to the podium to a loud applause.

He caught his reflection in the glass top of the wooden stand. He was dark–a rugged, youthful thirty-two with sharp green eyes and an intellect to match. With his tuft of thick black hair, strong jaw and taut features, female colleagues often told him he could pass for a model.

"Thank you," David said. He looked out over the audience and took a deep breath.

"Medicine, for all its progress, has not, at least in my opinion, made any giant leaps in the field of plastic surgery. Face-lifts, are done the same way as twenty years ago. Breast-implants, although vastly more popular, have changed little. They have more sophisticated equipment, the techniques, however, remain the same. I'm sure many of my colleagues sitting out there are challenged by this; that is my intent."

Several of the audience members looked stung by David's comments; their own practices' David knew, focused on practical applications of proven surgical techniques. David was implying these techniques were no longer valid.

A murmuring that emerged from the audience quieted.

"In the case of skin grafts for burn patients, they often endure dressing changes and treatments as painful as the burns they've suffered. That is, the ones who don't succumb to overwhelming infection. Fire burns many over ninety percent of their body, which leaves little intact skin to graft. Xenograft from swine runs the risk of passing a virus that could kill the patient. The current crop of lab-grown skin remains mediocre at best: a huge disappointment to the biotech companies who touted it as 'amazing,' then found themselves mired in bankruptcy when it didn't live up to expectations. The few companies that did survive, only manage to produce inferior quality skin that still requires sutures, and has an artificial look to it, which gives a mannequin-like appearance."

David put his hand on the podium and stared out at the audience. "Soon I expect to provide the medical community with a product that will make the experience of skin graft surgery something you have never imagined."

David's product proved nothing short of a miracle.

The scar free surgery allowed burn victims, regardless of their degree of injury, complete restoration to normal skin integrity. The initial trials, done on rats and mice, then, finally on a simian, proved to be truly remarkable. One well-known researcher observed, "It was as if the skin had grown from the existing flesh."

David's other advantage, unlike most biotech firms, was that his was not dependent on the ability to lure outside investors to finance it. He'd tapped into a little known government program that allowed a company to do their initial research with federal grants. The program only granted up to five million dollars, but David kept his company small, and only needed a small staff to produce the skin for his trials. At some point he knew, he would have to expand and take his company public. He was certain though, after the medical community saw the results, investors would fight to get a piece of his company. The first human trial would be ready the minute the FDA gave the green light.

After a slide presentation highlighting the finer points of his presentation, David stepped back to the podium.

"My final statement is this." David's demeanor turned cold and stiff, he felt slightly rebuffed by the audience. "As doctors we have taken an oath to heal. Sometimes our greatest nemesis is us. Our lack of imagination. Remember that medicine is not grander than the human mind. Should we not plum the depths of that imagination and find ways to outstrip mother nature? I think so. Will you be up to the challenge? I hope so. Thank You."

When David finished, applause echoed through the conference hall. He backed away from the podium surprised at the audience. Although it pleased his ego, it felt bittersweet. The one person who gave him the motivation to excel in his field could not be here to share the success with him.

The applause droned on and David let his mind drift back twenty years. *His mother had survived, but the fire forever changed her life.* Horribly disfigured, and too embarrassed to go out in public, she fell into a deep depression that kept her in bed most of the time. When she did get up, it would be to sit in front of her vanity mirror and stare at herself until she cried. Her once beautiful face now resembled melted wax. David tried to comfort and reassure her that he loved her with all his heart—which he did. Her depression, however, was more than anyone could fix. The human mind is capable of many emotions: happiness, sadness, despair, and grief. Then, there's something more grave and devastating. A feeling so deep, few people ever experience it. An overwhelming sense of loss that transcends all space and time. David's mother felt it, as David himself did. He had found her hunched over her vanity table. *A .38-caliber bullet buried in her brain, the gun still warm in her hand.* Her life extinguished in a single second.

The horror of that day faded, and David's gaze scanned the room for his colleagues. Many of which he knew, or had worked with at various stages of his career. He withdrew from the podium and stepped back.

Did they see what he tried so hard to hide?

Chapter Five

The symposium ended at four o'clock and David Reel stepped down and collected his notes. It was tempting to leave right away, but he knew it would mean driving through rush-hour traffic. Biding his time, and scanning the faces around him, David noticed an attractive brunette walking toward him. He admired her as she came closer.

With deep-set blue eyes and raven black hair that looked newly blown dry, she had a face any plastic surgeon would discourage altering. Trailing her was the faint scent of Johnson's Baby Powder. His eyes fell the length of her slender torso–to her white blouse and neatly pleated black skirt. He also felt a sense of deja vu.

"Dr. Reel." She extended her hand.

David's spirits lifted a little. "Yes. Have we met?"

"No, we haven't. I'm Jean Stokes. Your presentation was very impressive. It fascinated me."

"Thank you. I'll take that as a compliment. Are you a physician?"

"Oh no. I could never do that…what you do. The thought of slicing into someone with a scalpel…it makes me nauseous. I am, however, a researcher. Molecular Biology, actually."

"That's interesting. Where are you employed?"

She blinked; it seemed as though something opened up from within her.

"I was at Cal-Tech, but I've recently come to the east coast. Los Angeles got to be too hectic for me. I'm here in Washington to look for a position."

"Well, today could be your lucky day. It just so happens, Miss Stokes—"

"Please, call me Jean."

"As I was saying, Jean, it just so happens I'm looking for a lab assistant. Someone with a background in molecular biology."

"Really," Jean said.

"I'd like to sit and talk with you. Do you think you could come by my office tomorrow?" David asked.

"That would be fantastic."

"Okay, say around nine. Here, I'll write down directions for you."

As David finished packing, he felt a sense of accomplishment. He had let the medical community know his product was ready, and in the process, possibly found a lab assistant. His research was in a critical phase and he needed additional help. He had avoided hiring anyone unless absolutely necessary because of the sensitive nature of his work. With FDA approval just days away though, he had no choice.

Jean Stokes was a Ph.D. in cell biology and would make an excellent addition to David's team. Could he trust her though? That was the crucial question. Scientific espionage was not at all uncommon these days. Every biotech company scrambled to develop new products before the next guy could go public and gobble up another chunk of venture capital.

David felt good about her. Strange though, he felt like he had met her before. *Impossible, she had said.* She'd never been to the east coast.

The crowd had begun to disperse, and doctors headed back to their hotels to change for dinner. David spotted Jean Stokes and held the glass door open for her.

"I'll look forward to seeing you tomorrow," he said.

David stepped out into the afternoon shadows, crossing Wisconsin Avenue and heading for his car. He'd be back at the lab in half an hour. Then he had to get ready for an important appointment. He realized he was smiling for the first time all week.

That was some girl.

Chapter Six

If there is a bar on the way to Hell, it must look like the Taboo Lounge in Southeast, D.C.

David Reel gazed at it with quiet reservation. Outside, it was a fortification of iron-clad windows and doors, surrounded by the odor of urine and stale beer. A place where rent was cheap, and for the right price, you could get anything done.

David sighed, weighing his options. He'd never even been to this part of town, and by the looks of it, he hoped it would be the last time. *But what choice did he have?* He dodged two brown patches on the sidewalk, then hesitated as a couple of leather-clad trolls pawed past him. They eyed him, then his car that he'd parked across the street. Either man could have carried it away on his shoulders.

One of them peered over the top of his sunglasses at David. "You lookin for a score man?"

"No, I'm here to meet someone."

"Aren't we all?" the other troll grinned.

When the two went in without looking back, he felt relieved.

Opening the door and gazing in a minute later, he saw why they called it a biker-bar. There was enough leather apparel on everyone to upholster all the seats in a good size theater.

He collected his nerve and went in, then walked to the bar, avoiding all eye contact. He took out the card with the name of the guy: "Don," no last name given, just "Don." He was the one who would do it. No questions' asked–for a fee of course. David didn't care what it cost. He had waited long enough. *And the timing was crucial.*

David tapped his jacket pocket and assured himself he had the instructions for the guy. "Don" would have to follow them to the letter. When the bartender appeared out of the shroud of cigarette and other smoke that hung in the air, David looked up.

Was everyone here huge?

"What can I get you?" he asked David.

"I'm here to see Don."

"Who should I say wants' him?"

"Tell him it's Phil's friend," David said, raising his voice over the juke box blasting out AC/DC's *Highway to Hell.*

The bartender disappeared behind a makeshift partition made from a plastic shower curtain stretched over some thin plywood. Scanning the crowd, David saw small packages slide across the tables. It didn't take much imagination to know what was going on, and he felt the sooner he finished his own business and got out of there, the better. The last thing he needed was for the police to raid the place with him at the bar. That would be the end of his medical license, and his research. *Hurry up, Don.*

When Don did appear a few minutes later, he was not what David expected. In sharp contrast to the rest of the crowd, he was small and wiry. Stringy blond hair hung to his shoulders, tattoos covered his arms and seemed to merge into one perpetual design. David's trained eye went immediately to the scar that ran the length of his left cheek. *A scar that only a sharp object with ragged edges could have left.*

He could only imagine what had led to that. David felt sympathy for the man, as he did for anyone disfigured. He shook loose the thought. He was here for business.

Don introduced himself and extended his hand.

"I understand you have something you need done?"

David nodded. "Are you sure you can you handle it? It's not going to be easy."

"Listen, Dave. I can call you Dave can't I?" His smile revealed teeth in the advanced stages of periodontal disease.

David nodded again.

"As I said, Dave. If you've got the money, there isn't anything I can't do. Speaking of which, did you bring the money?"

David reached over and tapped his breast pocket. "How soon?"

"Tomorrow night. You got the instructions?"

"Yes, they're in with the money. Then you'll deliver them tomorrow night?"

"Late. More like early morning. It won't be any picnic."

"I understand. Then I'll just wait to hear from you."

"Good," Don said. "I'll call you when I'm ready to meet you. Now, about the money."

"Yes of course." David reached into his jacket pocket and produced a long brown envelope. It bulged in the front and Don smiled when he saw it. David slid it across the bar and it disappeared into Don's jacket as if he were Houdini.

"I'll talk to you later," Don said, and vanished behind the partition.

David turned and scanned the motley assortment of leather-clad patrons. Most lay stretched out in their chairs, in various stages of intoxication from their vice of choice.

Ignoring the curious stares, David took a deep breath and pushed through the curtain of smoke, straight out the door.

He hoped his car was still in the same place he'd left it.

Chapter Seven

"I don't understand, David," the engineer said.

Bannister Medical Inc. was David's main supplier for all his lab equipment. He had spent some five-million dollars in three years with them, so naturally they bent over backwards to satisfy him. However, when the chief engineer, who usually worked closely with David to make equipment to his specifications, got a request for a vacuum chamber, he called David.

"I'm not paying you to understand. I'm paying you to make equipment for me," David said.

David had given the engineer intimate details about his research, even though he was surreptitious with his work. The engineers needed to know details in order to make the equipment properly. David understood that. This, however, was different. He needed two vacuum chambers. No questions asked.

Previously, all his research revolved around the hyperbaric chamber: it pumped oxygen into the growing skin samples. Now, he wanted to suck oxygen out with a vacuum chamber. Obviously, the engineer didn't get it.

And David didn't want him to.

David shifted his weight and cradled the phone in his chin. "Just make the damn things. I don't have time to explain. You have the specs and the check. I need them in forty-eight hours."

"I'll get to work on them right away," the man said.

David slammed the phone down and went to the back of the lab. He unlocked the heavy reinforced door to the OFF LIMITS area. Behind it was a second door. Also reinforced and secured. David unlocked it with a special key and pulled it open. He stepped into the vaultlike room and flipped on the light. David scanned the interior and looked down. A maze of new plastic tubing ran the length of the floor and connected to a large holding tank of formaldehyde. He was pleased as he gazed at the new equipment. What he had dreamed of for years, finally seemed within his grasp.

He only needed two more things.

Chapter Eight

At the D.C.-Maryland line, the bus station provided a perfect spot for the bag lady to loiter. The police didn't seem to mind much, so long as she wasn't drunk and disorderly, or didn't panhandle too much. The bathroom was the one place a homeless person could actually feel at home. If no one was around, a spoon jammed into the sink faucet made a handy shower. Her favorite trick.

When she made her weekly pilgrimage into the ladies room for her clean up ritual she found her favorite sink cluttered. She looked around thinking someone else might be there, but it was only her.

"Now what do we have here?" she said out loud.

On the sink was a half-full bottle of hair dye: black, her own color. She looked in the mirror, and pushed the scarf back from her forehead revealing a mat of grey hair. "Yes sir, I can use this," she said to the mirror.

Under the sink was a plastic bag. She looked around again, grabbed up the bag and clung to it like a child protecting their last piece of Halloween candy. Inside the bag, someone had rolled up a tan sweater in a ball. For her, it was as good as a gold strike. Cold weather was coming, and winters in D.C. could be brutal. She stared at the sweater again and smiled. Curious about that name though. She'd never heard of a Shepard-Pratt. There it was though, right on the inside tag. It must be expensive? Someone had left a perfectly good sweater there. Too bad for them. It was hers now.

Chapter Nine

Don Spence was a career criminal. He'd started young, and there wasn't much he hadn't done for a fast buck, since. However, even criminals have principles, and his current job, for David Reel, violated even his. Despite his extensive criminal background—that included among other things—murder, his parents had raised him in a strict Catholic home. Some of that religion rubbed off on him, so he believed in good and evil, heaven and hell, and don't under any circumstances, disturb the dead. Unless of course someone is paying you five-thousand dollars. So much for principle. Money or not, it still gave him the creeps.

The sound of his stolen, Blue Chevy van broke the stillness of the night as it passed under the gates of St. Mary's cemetery. The van stopped and Spence turned on a flashlight. He looked at the crudely-drawn map, then looked up.

"Drive over there," he said to Vinnie Delgado. "Over there on the right. I see it."

He turned off the flashlight. The old caretaker might spot them from the shack where he sat at night. Some surveillance the night before gave Spence that bit of information. He could see a light on, but the old man was probably asleep. The moon was full and the headstones cast narrow purple shadows across the cemetery.

Vinnie pulled behind a row of hedges and killed the engine. "Hurry up, let's get going."

"Just hold on a minute," Spence said. "I gotta see something." He looked out the window and saw the mausoleum he was looking for, just to the right of the gates. That would be the easy part. Digging up a grave would be a bitch.

Just keep thinking of the money.

Chapter Ten

The lab technician at the National Institute of Health was running at top speed, flying through the door he'd entered to the lab, down the short corridor, then turning, back down the long one to the elevator. Sweat beads flew off his forehead and his heart was pounding. He climbed to the elevator and descended to the basement. The elevator car smelled of freshly sprayed disinfectant. *No germicidal could kill this!*

The door parted and he hit the hall running again. He burst into his supervisor's office, his breath coming in ragged gasps.

"You need...to...come to the lab...now!"

A minute earlier he had flipped on the light switch in his lab and immediately sensed something wrong. Working isolated for long hours every night, he was intimately familiar with his surroundings. The long row of petri dishes that normally filled his peripheral vision each time he worked, *had vanished.*

These particular petri dishes contained samples of a lethal strain of bacteria, cultured from the skin of a patient in Columbia Medical Center a week earlier.

Now, returning to the lab, the tech yanked the paperwork from the file cabinet and thrust it at his supervisor. The narrative on the ER report was clear:

The patient, a 45-year-old construction worker, had been admitted to Columbia with an arm lesion the size of a half-dollar, and growing by the hour. After the infectious disease doctor examined the man, he had quietly walked out of the exam room and commented to his colleague, "Let's wait for the cultures to come back, but if it's what I think it is, it won't make any difference what we do."

The supervisor handed the file back to the lab tech. The color had drained from his face and he swallowed hard. "You better get the CDC on the phone. God help us if we don't find those petri dishes."

Chapter Eleven

The view of the Washington skyline from Key Bridge was beautiful at 3:00 A.M. Don Spence tried to see, but it had started to rain and he needed to watch the road. Spence was now behind the wheel of the stolen Chevy van headed toward Rockville. Vinnie Delgado sat in the front passenger seat, staring out the window. Both men were wearing gloves.

"Good view," Vinnie said. "I can see the Washington Monument."

"Yeah, I've seen it."

Vinnie turned toward Spence. "What's buggin you?"

"I don't like this job," Spence said. "Reminds me of *Tales From the Crypt* or some shit."

"The hard part is over, the rest is a cake walk."

"Not if we get caught."

Vinnie frowned. "We're not gonna get caught."

"You better hope not."

Vinnie glanced over at Don's scarred face silhouetted in the dim light of the van's interior.

"What do you mean?"

"Just this doctor, he gives me the creeps."

Vinnie laughed. "Yeah, I'm glad he's not my doctor."

"You're not funny, Vinnie."

"All right!" Vinnie said with resignation.

Spence maintained the speed limit. It got nerve racking riding with Vinnie and worrying about the cops stopping them. *How would he explain the two boxes?* He exited the parkway onto Randolph Road, then headed west into Rockville. The environment quickly changed from franchise fast-food restaurants to the heart of the industrial section. "You got the map and address out?" Spence asked.

" I got it right here," Vinnie said. He reached up and turned on the map light. "We're looking for Twinbrook Industrial Center. It'll be on the right."

Twinbrook Industrial Center proved easy to find. Five minutes later, massive brick buildings on both sides surrounded them.

"I don't like this," Spence said. "It's too quiet. We're going to stick out like a sore thumb."

"Just relax," Vinnie said. "There it is over there."

"What number is it?"

Vinnie consulted the piece of paper in his hand. "We're looking for seventeen. This is fifteen, here. It's two buildings down."

A few moments later, Spence slowed and pulled into the parking lot. Halogen lamps lined the front of the massive brick building. A few of the windows were aglow with light. The place was the size of a shopping center. Spence drove around to the back of the building.

Vinnie pointed to the overhead door with the large R painted on it. "This must be the place," he said.

"Yea, well let's just get this done and get out of here. This gives me the creeps," Spence said.

Vinnie frowned "You already said that."

The moon reflected off the only car in the parking lot, a blue BMW. Spence recognized it as David Reel's.

They parked, then stepped out of the van just as the overhead door rolled up. Vinnie yanked open the van's rear doors revealing two wooden crates, each one six feet by three feet. Both were marked: FRAGILE.

The two men watched in silence as a figure descended onto the loading dock.

"Let's get this over with," Spence said, stepping up to meet Reel.

"All right. Just be careful getting them off," David Reel said.

"We got them this far didn't we?" Vinnie said.

The three of them unloaded the crates and set them in the back of the lab. Spence gazed at the two big metal containers with curved glass tops parked in the middle of the room. On each one, BANNISTER MEDICAL had emblazoned its logo across the

31

rocketlike hull in blue letters. A winding maze of tubes ran from the tops of each one and snaked across the floor. It was unlike anything he'd ever seen.

"What kind of shit are you doing here anyway, doc?"

"Nothing you would understand," David Reel said.

Spence shook his head. "You truly are a weird guy. And they told me *I* was fucked up. Well, it's been a pleasure doing business with you, doc. Let's go Vinnie."

* * *

David closed the overhead door. *It was anything but a pleasure doing business with those two low lifes.* Was he any better though, considering what he had done? He put it out of his mind and looked at the two wooden crates.

"I have work to do."

Chapter Twelve

The next morning, Jean Stokes arrived at David Reel's office for her interview. She was twenty minutes early and again impressed David.

"I almost missed it," Jean said.

"If you're not looking for it, you can pass it right by," David said. "Most of the adjoining buildings are primarily, storage. I like the privacy it affords me."

Jean held up her hands. "Anyway, I made it."

David hoped Jean didn't expect a fancy office. His taste in office furnishings ran more to the ordinary. A gray metal desk with a white Formica top, gray metal file cabinet, a small etagere for books, a couple of pictures, and two chrome chairs for visitors. The only indulgence he could claim was his own chair. A brown plush recliner where David often slept. It almost looked out of place with the rest of the office, but it was the epitome of comfort for him. His mother had passed it along and he had re-covered it several times over the years. "Let's sit in my office."

Jean Stokes mesmerized David. Her dark hair, pulled back tight, gave her a studious look one would expect of a woman with a Ph.D. in cell biology.

David began the interview by explaining the focus of his research, and how Reel Skin would be on the market in a matter of months.

"I'm slowly gearing up for surgery again. I only see patients in my office Monday and Wednesday, and I only operate on Thursday."

Jean Stokes nodded. "What I want to know is, how can I help? I'd really like to be part of your team."

David tapped a pencil on the desk. "I need someone to manage the lab while I devote more time to screening potential patients for the first human trials."

"I'd really like to be that person," Jean said.

"You certainly have the credentials. I'll just need to do a background check."

"I understand. You can't be too careful these days."

"I tell you what though. How would you like a tour of the lab?"

"That would be great."

A smile formed across her face, and David suddenly got the strangest feeling. "I don't mean to be coy, Jean, but, are you sure we've never met before? You seem vaguely familiar."

"I get that a lot, but no, we haven't met. I'm sure I would remember."

David walked Jean Stokes through the lab, taking extra time to show her the hyperbaric chambers where hundreds of skin samples were in various stages of growth. They filled one half of the front lab, while a bank of computers that constantly monitored the process, filled the wall on the other side of the room. Several high definition microscopes sat on a maze of lab tables. The animal room, where David had a collection of rats and mice, as well as his prized baboon, Dexter, was in a separate room to the right of the lab.

Then there was the OFF LIMITS area, where David allowed no one except himself. No other person ever entered that part of the lab. David informed every employee it would be grounds for dismissal should they even talk about it. The last lab tech who had pressed David about what it contained, found himself unemployed the next day. No one dare mention it since.

Jean Stokes seemed genuinely fascinated with the lab despite her apparent experience in the field. David found that to be a desirable trait in an employee. If they were enthusiastic and curious. *But not too curious.* David hoped her background check would not reveal anything to keep him from hiring her.

He really liked this girl.

Chapter Thirteen

"God dammit, lieutenant. Why do I get stuck with this whacko?" Holland Carters' voice boomed across his boss's desk.

"Because you're the best man for the job. Unless of course you'd like to work vice with Hobbs."

Carter stood up, his massive bulk dwarfing the bantam lieutenant. "No, that's all right. I'll handle this."

"Get back to me as soon as you find out something," the lieutenant said, "And check with Hobbs, she can fill you in."

The Missing Shepard Pratt Arsonist Case, as the Baltimore Sun and other local newspapers called it, was now Carter's problem. *Just great.* While the hospital stonewalled behind confidentiality rules designed to protect the patient–but in this case to cover their own ass—the girl in question vanished.

There were no leads in the case.

Gernine Hobbs sat at her desk studying a case file when Carter walked up. She was a stocky black woman with a close-cropped Afro.

"Hobbs. Do you have the file on this girl from Shepard Pratt?"

"I'm looking at it now. She's one crazy bitch."

"I hear she's different?"

Hobbs leaned back in her chair. "Oh yeah. She is that. She's not your garden variety sociopath, if that's what you mean. She has a huge I.Q. That should make it a challenge for you, Carter."

"That's funny, Hobbs. You sure you don't want to handle this?"

"No, I've got my hands full with half-dead winos."

Carter took the file from Hobbs and looked at what they had so far: She was a white female, twenty-six-years-old, red hair, blue eyes, and one-hundred-twenty pounds on a five-foot-seven frame. They put her away six years ago after a California court found her guilty by reason of insanity, for burning down her college dormitory at California Technical Institute where she majored in molecular biology. Twenty-four of her fellow coeds perished in the fire. All died a horrible death: *literally roasted alive.* Many woke up at the last minute to find themselves engulfed in flames.

Carter leaned on the edge of Hobb's desk. "I remember reading about this case a long time ago."

"It's a tragic story, Carter, but anyone who could barbecue twenty-four of her fellow students and not show the least bit of remorse at her trial, is one scary bitch."

Carter pondered that. What would possess a young woman with a brilliant mind to commit such a heinous crime? He understood insanity, with all it's chemical imbalances and scientific explanations. He could grasp that idea. He'd sent enough criminals to Shepard Pratt himself during his career. Still, what in God's name could have happened to this girl?

Carter closed the folder and turned to go.

"Good luck," Hobbs said.

Chapter Fourteen

Light rain, almost a mist. A soft whispering envelope that cloaked everything in velvety gray.

The quiet Catholic churchyard with rhododendron bushes under spreading elms. Worn writing on old tombstones and the sweet smell of freshly mown grass. The yawning seven-by-three-foot grave, its dark earth damp. The coffin bronze and covered with flowers waiting to be lowered. A young boy next to quiet mourners with somber faces, dark clothes.

"Earth to earth, ashes to ashes, dust to dust, in sure and certain hope of the resurrection to eternal life." And afterward, dry sandwiches, tea, coffee, and sherry at the rectory to fortify those weakened by the immediate presence of death–untimely death which made their own urgently imminent.

At no point had it ever crossed the mind of any who participated in the funeral that the body which occupied the grave in front of them would ever be anything but permanently entombed in the sealed confines of the cold bronze coffin. Not even himself.

"Dr. Reel?" A voice that persisted. "Dr. Reel."

David was still in his office at the Medical Pavilion and it was after 10:00 P.M. He finally looked away from the picture. One of the security guards stood in the doorway. It was the night watchman from the lobby door downstairs.

"If I'm not at my desk when you want to check out I'll be back in ten minutes. I'm just going for coffee."

"Sure," David said.

The guard disappeared. David was alone again.

He gazed back at the picture. The images stared at him and gave him no answer. He turned it face down and rose from his desk. When he got up, his hands were shaking uncontrollably. He couldn't come to terms with what he'd done.

It was too unbelievable.

Chapter Fifteen

The enormous iron gates of Shepard Pratt were like a descent into purgatory for Holland Carter.

The institution was a collection of four-story stone buildings built in 1920. Oak trees a hundred-years-old cast gigantic shadows across the slate roof, giving it the look of an Ivy League college. Ahead, the casual atmosphere gaveway to armed guards stationed at the entrance, and reminded him that the place housed some of the most dangerous criminals that ever lived.

Carter approached the front door of the main building and flashed his badge. The guard thanked him, then pushed a button and let him pass inside. He came to another guard on the inside where a sliding door closed in the middle and separated the entrance from the main hospital. He got directions to the administrator's office, then passed through the second door. A few Thorazine zombies wandered about, thick tongued and catatonic. Carter ignored them.

Kay Allworth looked as though she were expecting him when he got to her office.

"Good morning, officer. I've gotten everything we have on her for you."

Carter looked around, then pushed the door closed.

"Look lady, cut the crap. First of all it's, Detective. Second, I don't really care what you have. I'm going to search her room from top to bottom. While I'm doing that I suggest you get *all* her records together. Not just what you want to show me. Then, we'll talk about what you have."

"Our own security has already searched the room."

"Did you hear what I said? I don't care. I'm going to search it again."

"Yes of course. I'll have an orderly show you to the room, Detective."

A few minutes later, an orderly opened the huge steel-door to the room. It hung on hinges as big as railroad spikes, and it reminded him of how old the place really was. Modern facilities have hydraulic doors that slide on a track. Time had apparently passed Shepard Pratt by.

The decor was simple and pleasant. The walls were a pastel green, with woodwork the same color only a darker shade. Beige linen curtains hid the bars in the single window, and a goose-down comforter the same color as the curtains covered the twin bed. A white wicker bureau and matching desk were the only other pieces of furniture in the room. A small Oku lithograph, of a girl on a boat, hung above the bed.

"Pretty pleasant room," Carter said. *Pretty pleasant, considering the former occupant was insane.*

Allworth walked in. "She decorated it herself. Shepard Pratt encourages all its patients to decorate their room as they please. Provided it's done in good taste."

Carter imagined that was the idea of the resident shrink, who felt it was therapeutic to let them express their personality–or more accurately–*one of their personalities.*

The room appeared as if a well-adjusted individual had decorated it. Had she decorated it to reflect what lie just beneath the surface of her personality, Carter imagined, she would would have painted the walls fire engine red, with smoke gray curtains and bedspread. Copies of Pyromaniac's Monthly would be arranged on the bureau next to the can of her favorite accelerant.

Like everything else at Shepard Pratt though, they only let you see things that give the illusion of success. *In fact, no one ever left there—sane.*

Carter, satisfied that he had seen enough, was about to leave, when he spotted *it*. Just the corner stuck out, so he almost missed it. He lifted the stack of sweaters from the closet shelf. The girl apparently had a thing for sweaters judging by the number of them.

Underneath, he found a standard dime-store scrapbook. Vinyl bound, with gold-leaf embossed letters across the front: MEMORIES. He examined it carefully. Each page turned, revealed some new aspect of the girl. Pictures, newspaper articles, some dating back twenty-years, some, of which he remembered. A few letters never mailed, a few post cards partially addressed. Each one a sad memory of a tragic life. When he finished, one thing became clear: at one time, she had been a normal kid.

Carter's face softened. "I'll need to take this," he said.

Allworth nodded. "Anything else?"

"I'll be in touch."

Chapter Sixteen

"I hate this!" David said aloud. He sat by himself in the glass enclosed office of his expansive lab. At his desk he had no less than a hundred applications spread out in front of him.

It was a difficult task: deciding who to accept, and who he would have to turn down. He'd agonized for days over what criteria to use. They were all worthy applicants.

The FDA had made it clear though, three patients initially. Then, if all went well, he would have carte blanche. The problem for David was right in front of him; he had received literally hundreds of requests to be involved in the trials. Physicians as far away as Germany had contacted him wanting to know how they could get their patients into the program. Unfortunately, he had to narrow it down to the mere three the FDA had agreed to. Every request was for a severely burned patient that required extensive skin grafts.

David looked beyond those damaged exteriors and into the human faces beneath them. He poured over the applications, each story more heart wrenching than the last. It also churned up painful memories of his own tragic past.

Finally, after procrastinating for hours, he decided on three patients. One, a small child, badly burned when he pulled a pot of boiling water from the stove onto himself, would be the only child in the trials. The other two, a woman in her thirties, burned in a car wreck, and a forty-year-old man, horribly disfigured when his plane crashed, troubled David the most. Their histories fit the criteria he had set up, based on their general health, previous grafts, and mental state.

Even though he could only pick three, the FDA assured him they that would give him final approvals soon as the initial results proved successful. In fact, once his product was on the market, he would train other plastic surgeons in his technique. Reel Skin would be available to everyone.

David's conscience had begun to bother him. He felt a tinge of guilt for lying to the FDA. They agreed to approve the initial trials based on the results of the animal tests. David tried to do things by the book, but when it came to the FDA, more often than not, they erred on the side of safety, at the expense of people who needed new products and medicines immediately. So he fudged his data to speed things up and claimed his animal trials were over. The truth was, the results weren't in yet—they were another two weeks out.

Conscience or not, he felt he'd waited long enough. Besides, who were they to tell him whether his product was safe or not. They only knew what he told them anyway. It was safe, and he'd already proved it by trying it on himself. He felt confident enough to go ahead with the surgeries; what the FDA didn't know wouldn't hurt them.

That—it seemed—had become his motto for everyone, lately.

Chapter Seventeen

Two weeks after he'd submitted Jean Stoke's background check to Interfax Security, David Reel grew impatient. He still hadn't heard anything. Now that he had FDA approval, he needed someone to run the lab while he did the work-ups on his trial patients. *Trial* was an understatement. It was language used to make it appeal to the FDA's board. These were actual surgeries that would require a great deal of skill and concentration. David couldn't preoccupy himself with the lab. *At least during the day.* With her background, Jean Stokes would be perfect to run it.

He picked up the phone and placed a call to the agency. After one ring, a pleasant female voice answered. "Interfax Security, may I help you?"

"Yes, this is Dr. Reel. I submitted an application for a background check on a potential employee a couple of weeks ago, and I was wondering if it was completed yet?"

"What was the name of the person?"

"Jean Stokes."

"Just a minute, I'll check."

Do You Know the Way to San Jose? filled the line while David waited. Elevator music to calm the impatient. *He liked it better by Dion Warwick.*

The girl came back on the line. "Dr. Reel. That's being handled by Dick Olson. I'll transfer you to his office."

David had met Dick Olson once before when he was setting up his lab. David remembered his surprise at Olson's appearance. Olson—head investigator at Interfax, was a loping stick figure of a man. His gaunt six-foot frame resembled a collection chicken bones strung together. Above his precarious body was a jaundiced face whose skin was a sheet of wrinkled parchment paper accented by two drooping eyes. At fifty-two, he looked seventy.

Olson was tenacious though when it came to his job. They revered him in Washington as a god in the security business. They said that given the chance, he could garner Mother Teresa herself, a skeleton or two from her closet.

The song ended and another elevator tune started, but Olson picked up just in time to spare David a harpsichord version of *It's Not Unusual.*

"Dr. Reel?"

"Yes."

"Dick Olson, how've you been. I'm handling the background check you requested."

"Fine," David said, "how's it coming?"

"Well, I've completed the first part, and the good news is, nothing came up on the NCIC computer. So we know there's no criminal record."

David sat forward in his chair. "You said, *good news.* Does that mean there's bad news as well?"

Olson laughed a little. "I'm sorry, Dr. Reel. I didn't mean to infer that. It's just that I know you stated on your application that you were in a hurry, but it's probably going to take another week or so to get her records from Cal Tech. They're very protective over there. Lot of red tape to go through."

"Well isn't there some way to speed up the process? I don't have two weeks."

"Unfortunately not. I'm at the mercy of the folks who release the information, and with all the confidentiality laws today, it just takes time."

David let out a long breath. "I see."

"I'll do what I can to speed things along, but I still think your looking at probably ten more days."

"All right. Please call me the minute you hear something."

David hung up and slapped his hand on the arm of the chair. "Damn."

He needed the help, yet he wanted to be sure that the people he hired were clean. Olson did say she didn't have a criminal record, and that's the main thing to worry about. Maybe he would hire her on the strength of that. Under the circumstances, he didn't see any other way. He could always fire her later if any derogatory information came back.

David picked up Jean Stokes employment application and dialed her number.

"Hello," Jean answered.

"Jean, David Reel. Could you come by the office? I have some good news."

Chapter Eighteen

Jean Stokes arrived at David's lab 7:00 A.M. sharp. She let herself in with the key he'd given her the day before, and it startled her to see him sprawled across his desk asleep.

"David, are you all right?"

He slowly raised himself, squinting at the daylight that poured through the skylights.

"Jean, oh jeez. I must have fallen asleep. I worked late last night. Trying to catch up on last minute details."

"Anything I can do to help?"

"No!…No," David said.

"I'm sorry, just trying to help."

"No, I'm sorry, Jean. It's just a lot of pressure right now. I don't mean to be cross with you. Besides, I haven't had my morning coffee yet." David let a smile form.

"I can fix that. Here you go. Double cappuccino, just like you like it."

"How'd you know that?"

"I'm a good listener, remember?"

Jean impressed David. A thing as simple as his preference for coffee, and she remembered. And *once again, he felt that familiarity he couldn't place. Where?*

David took the coffee then stood up and stretched. "Well, I guess you're anxious to get to work," he said.

"Yes, but I must admit I'm a little nervous. I've never worked on such an important project."

"No need to be nervous. Come over here and let me show you the skin matrix chamber. That's where you'll do most of your work."

David stood back as Jean surveyed one of the hyperbaric chambers where he was now producing Reel Skin at a furious pace. The chamber was a huge stainless steel tank with a door like a walk-in refrigerator. He stepped up and opened the door. Inside, racks spaced ten inches apart, went from bottom to top. Each rack contained a stainless flat pan that held a sheet of growing skin 12 inches square.

David pulled one out. "Kinda like making Creepy Crawlers as a kid," he said.

"That's amazing," Jean said.

David pushed the tray back in and closed the door. "What I'll need you to do, is to monitor the daily growth rate. When each tray reaches the perimeter of the pan, remove it and examine it for any unusual characteristics. If it's perfect, then you'll store it in a bath of saline until we need it."

"That doesn't sound too hard."

"It's not. But that's only part of it. The other thing you'll be doing is actually mixing the components of the skin. This is where your molecular biology comes in."

David led Jean to the rear of the lab. Passing an area marked, OFF LIMITS, Jean looked at David.

"What's in there?"

David turned bright red. "Nothing your job has anything to do with." He abruptly turned away. "Now as I was saying, the other part of your job will be mixing the matrix."

They stopped at a small bank of computers. A clear glass vat sat next to them where tubes ran from the vat into a gray box that connected to a port on the computer.

"This is a Matrix Spectrometer," David said. He put his hand on top of it as if it were a pet. "It registers the amount of each component used to make the skin. You'll need to calculate the amounts based on the thickness you want. After the formula is correct, the computer will add the exact amounts for you. Then it goes to the hyperbaric chamber. I'll run you through a simulation later today so you can get a feel for it. Any questions?"

"I'm sure I'll think of plenty before the day's out, but for now I'm confused enough."

"Don't worry," David said, "I'm sure you'll pick it up in no time. And speaking of time, I need to get to the office. Just familiarize yourself with the equipment, and I'll be back later. If you need anything, Cindy can help you."

David left feeling satisfied he'd done the right thing hiring Jean. Security check or not, she was intelligent and would catch on quickly.

He only wished the nagging feeling that he knew her would go away.

Chapter Nineteen

After David Reel had familiarized her with the lab, Jean Stokes had spent the next few days going over her plan. Her past six years of exile had prepared her well for what was to come. She'd devoured every issue of Journal of Molecular Biology–the industry newsletter, which they mailed to her monthly. She'd spent every waking minute thinking of David Reel. It had occupied her time, and as always dominated her thinking. Next week it would all pay off. She could hardly believe she was face to face with the bastard.

Now that she had put the wheels in motion, a sense of calm settled over her. She had a lot to do in the next five days. A bus ticket to buy, some appearance alterations to plan. More study to do.

She took the floppy disk David gave her and loaded it into the computer. When the program was ready, she pushed a command:

ADD COMPONENTS: SR-21 PLUS UNKNOWN MATERIAL

The screen gave a prompt:

UNKNOWN MATERIAL ACCEPTED–RUN BATCH #00949

The computer hummed and started processing. They designed the machine to add whatever skin components the operator programed in for each particular batch. Any organic compounds could be loaded into the spectrometer fill tank. You could add virtually anything to the mix without changing the basic structure. Thus, you could add certain melanin pigments to produce black skin, or add less to make a lighter shade. David had thought of everything Jean observed.

Except what she had added.

She went to the incubator and began to store the sheets of skin. She had to give David credit. The material was truly amazing. It was as natural as anyone's actual skin could be. As she stored one of the sheets away, a custodian David occasionally used held some petri dishes in his hand and looked at Jean.

"Are these yours?" he asked, holding up one of the dishes with red gel in the center.

"Oh yes, thank you. I was just going to run some tests with some different reagents. I'll take them, thanks."

Jean took the four containers and slipped them in the side pocket of her lab jacket. *Got to be more careful!*

Their contents were rare.

Chapter Twenty

David got home just before dawn and made a pot of strong coffee. He carried a mug into the bedroom and sipped the steaming brew while he undressed and prepared to get a shower. His case load was light today, a fact he was especially grateful to Paul for, given David's current state of fatigue.

By the time he turned down Wisconsin Avenue an hour later, a light drizzle had shined the streets. His work so preoccupied him, he didn't notice the rain until someone crossed the street in front of him holding an umbrella.

At the first red light, David took the opportunity to look at his appointment book. One rhinoplasty at ten, then at eleven, a suture removal from a breast augmentation he had done a week earlier. *Perfect.* That would leave him the rest of the day for the lab. After this week, he'd not be seeing anyone except his trial patients. This had elicited several complaints from repeat clients. Ruth Epstein wanted her yearly face lift, but David, much to her protest, had referred her to Paul Gallo. He doubted if she even had any skin left to stretch. They'd pulled her eyes so tight now she'd soon have nothing but peripheral vision left.

David parked in the Medical Arts Pavilion garage, then dashed right in past the security guard. He stopped at the elevator long enough to push the button just as the door opened. When he got to his office he plopped down in his chair a blew a ragged breath. It seemed fatigue was his permanent partner lately, and he wondered if he would ever get some decent sleep again.

He reached across the desk and picked up the picture he had placed there when he opened his practice five years ago. It was an old picture, but it was his favorite.

In a happier place and time, it showed David as an eleven-year-old boy, standing next to his mother, an attractive brunette. To David she was vibrant, *alive.*

Now, his only peace and sanity came from *those* days much farther back in time....his childhood, the years when his mother and Sam had been his whole life. David drew those memories around him now. He gazed back at the picture.

The ocean in the background, a sand castle in front of them, it was one of the happiest times of his life. His week at the beach with his mom. He would have never dreamed that only one short year later, a tragedy, too horrifying to contemplate, would take her. The world is no place for motherless children, he remembered thinking while his own suicide waited to swallow him up. But he didn't. Because of her. He owed her at least that much.

David held the picture close to him. "Don't worry," he whispered.

Concentrating as deeply as he was, it startled David when the phone on his desk rang. He wiped tears away then picked up the receiver.

Why hadn't his secretary answered it?

"Hello. This is Dr. Reel."

"David, it's Jean."

"Jean...is anything wrong?"

Chapter Twenty One

That night, with Jean gone from the lab, David went to the supply cabinet and grabbed a surgical mask. It was not for antiseptic purposes. It was purely because he didn't know what to expect in the next few minutes.

Plastic surgery was a complicated process. Part science, part art, it required an intricate knowledge of human anatomy and physiology. David possessed all the skill required to make him one of the best and brightest in his field. Since graduating at the top of his class at Johns Hopkins, David used a scalpel like Michelangelo used a paint brush. He maintained an inner drive as if some unseen specter obsessed him.

What he was doing now though, would challenge even his skills, and push him to the brink emotionally.

It was the only thing in the world capable of eliciting his passion. It was his lifeline back to what he once had been.

He secured the lab and went to the OFF LIMITS door and slipped the key in the lock. The door swung open. There was nothing in the featureless metal to hint at what lay inside. David quickly stepped in and closed it. The only sound came from the wind hissing against the windows. He felt his nervousness swell.

The light switch made an inordinately loud snap when he turned it on. Banks of fluorscent light bathed the huge room. A central counter ran half of it, complete with gas jets, sink, and overlying shelves of laboratory glassware. At the far end was a surgery area, which looked like a small operating room. A gigantic kettle light hung over the surgical field. A vacuum pump stood silent beside it. Next to that sat the two recently delivered crates like two quiet observers. With every second that passed David's anxiety continued to increase.

He went to the first crate.

He found they'd only fastened it with some framing wire and a couple of finishing nails. He slid the top off easily. A layer of dry ice covered a plastic sheet and frigid air wrapped itself around David like a milky ghost. Under the plastic, a thick gelatinous membrane covered what lie beneath. With hands shaking, he pulled back the membrane.

David's legs buckled as he stared raptly into the box. Nothing could have prepared him for this. He had planned this day for years, and yet, instead of elation–it was like a nightmare—but there was no waking from this! *A horrible unnatural coldness that merged with the chill of the grave—and the odor of death long past.*

A flood of images exploded: his life, his mother, Sam, Jean....*Jean?*

Finally, he closed it. Terrified.

He composed himself, then stepped away and prepared the first of the two vacuum chambers. It was identical in structure to the second, with one exception: it was slightly longer.

They had arrived just as requested. The chief engineer had not probed any further about their use. It wasn't his business anyway.

David turned on the vacuum pump to the first chamber. It came to life with an electrical hum and began to hiss as it pumped the air out. *The perfect environment for preservation.*

It was already 5:00 A.M., too late to start the next phase. He needed to get to Washington General at nine to give a lecture. The hospital had been gracious in offering their assistance in the trial of Reel Skin, and David agreed to give the Board of Directors an overview of what to expect as well as their role in the trial surgeries.

David blew a tired breath and looked in the second crate. It would have to wait. He ran a hand through his oily hair, a result of being up for 36 hours straight. He stared at the lab.

Would his obsession become his undoing?

Not one given easily to melodrama, as David prepared to lock up, he looked at the vacuum chambers and the rest of the lab equipment. An old movie he had watched as a kid came to mind. It was the 1930 version–of *Frankenstein.*

Chapter Twenty Two

David Reel dragged himself up the stairs, the weight of the night pressing on him. When he went through the doors of Washington General, he felt like he'd just stepped off a bad carnival ride. The trip down Connecticut Avenue was a nightmare as usual, and fighting traffic only added to his exhaustion. Fatigue, disgust, elation, all bottled up inside of him. *Would he even remember what to say to the board?*

Although he originally wanted to use Johns Hopkins as his home base, recently they had come under fire, after several deaths in one of their drug trials. The last thing David needed was controversy or negative association, so he opted for Washington General. They had a great reputation and all the support staff he would need.

David went to the lobby and met Paul in front of the Starbucks machine. He and Paul enjoyed their daily coffee routine. They began each morning with a quiet cup as they planned the day and shared surgical stories.

"Hello, Paul."

Paul scanned David from head to toe. "David, what'd you do, sleep in your car?"

"Is it that bad?"

"Pretty bad, you all right?"

"Yeah, these trials are a lot of work."

"You know if you need any help, I'll be glad to rearrange some cases to give you a hand. I'm rootin for you."

"Two more days. It's been a long road, but final–"

"Dr. Reel. How are you?" the hospital administrator, Jeffery Vorrell, asked. He ignored Paul Gallo and gave David the once over.

David smiled, but noticed the look.

"Dr. Reel, If you do not mind me saying so, you look awfully tired. We can do this meeting later if you like."

"No, that's okay. It's just been a long week. I'm fine."

David finished drawing his coffee from the metal decanter, then excused himself. He never had the best relationship with Vorell, a mealy mouth little man who had an annoying habit of constantly clearing his throat. Since David announced his intentions of using Washington General for his trial surgeries, however, Vorell had treated David as nothing less than royalty. David kept his distance though. He was keen on the man's patronizing.

With a half hour still left till the meeting, David decided to go visit Charlie. He climbed on the elevator and descended to the basement.

Washington General was one of the first hospitals built in the city. Although renovated many times over the years and brought up to standard with the most modern hospitals, it seemed they forgot the basement. Going there was like a trip back in time, some even claimed World War I casualties who died there, still walked its halls. Here, in the very bowels of the hospital, antiquated cast-iron heating and water pipes, long since abandoned, stood alongside shiny new aluminum ducts. Anyone over five-nine ran the risk of head injury from the incredible maze. Lighting was sparse, accomplished by a few wire-covered sixty-watt bulbs placed at random intervals. Every time David came down here to visit Charlie, he wondered how the man could stand to work in this dungeon of pipes and wires.

Charlie Goodman was there the night it happened. A volunteer fireman with the Rock Creek Fire Company #6, his was the first to respond to the five-alarm fire on Gilbert Road. When he heard David's screams, he ran in the back of the house, risking his own life to grab him and pull him to safety just as the back draft blew through the house like a nuclear detonation.

While David was in the hospital, it was Charlie who would visit him every day. Soon, they developed a bond to last a lifetime. Charlie became the father David so desperately wanted. And when that awful day came and David's mother could no longer cope, and took her life, it was Charlie who adopted David and raised him. Still, despite Charlie's best efforts, David fell into a deep depression much like his mother had. David blamed himself for his mother's death. No physciatrist could convince him otherwise. No amount of therapy could erase the guilt. It was he who had given Sam the cigarette. But finally, it was Charlie Goodman who was able to lift David from the fog of despair he'd lived in for three long years. David had an affection for Charlie, although there were still times when David wished that they had not saved him. Charlie was always there for David no matter what. David occasionally slipped in and out of depression, but Charlie always seemed to pull him out of it. *Do it for your mother he would say.*

Finally, it was Charlie who recognized David's aptitude for science, encouraging him to go into medicine. David saw it as a way to make up for what happened to his mother and best friend. *Perhaps he could save others?* Charlie paid for David's education, using his own retirement money.

Now, Charlie was slowing, after being a maintenance engineer at Washington General for thirty years. David wanted to make sure Charlie had everything he needed in his old age. David felt he owed him that much.

As David gazed on the old walls, he remembered catching the bus to come see Charlie, then walk around the hospital, always curious, always asking questions. Dreaming that someday he would walk these halls as a doctor. *Funny how things come full circle.*

Charlie smiled when David walked up. He raised one of his mountain sized hands and patted him on the arm. "Davey, you look tired, son."

"You too, huh?"

"No, I'm not tired," Charlie said. "I just got up."

"No, I mean you see it too. You're the third person in as many minutes who has told me that."

"Maybe you need to slow down."

"I wish I could. There's just too much to do."

Charlie leaned back in his old leather office chair. "Talk around the hospital is that you're getting ready to do something very important."

The fatigue left David's eyes. "Charlie, I finally perfected my product. Now I can help all those people I've wanted to for so long."

"That's great, son. Just don't let it run you in the ground. Get some sleep once in a while. I've called you five times this week and never got an answer."

"I've been working late."

"Like I said, get some sleep or you may be the one who needs a doctor. You know what happened before."

"I'm way beyond that, Charlie. That was years ago."

Charlie had a point. Doctors had told David there might come a time when he could have a post-traumatic stress disorder, given the right circumstances. David felt he could judge for himself. *After all, he was a doctor.*

"Just be careful, Davey. You know I love you."

"I love you too, Charlie. Do you need anything?"

"Nothing I can think of."

"All right. I'll call you later. I've got to get to a meeting."

"See what I mean. Always have to be somewhere."

How true that was, David thought

David knew he could never tell Charlie the truth. It would hurt him too much. He wouldn't understand what went on behind those lab doors late at night. *No one would.*

One thing was certain though. If David Reel risked a relapse, his obsession had already pushed him beyond that point. But it was too late to stop.

Chapter Twenty Three

David felt a precarious uncertainty as he emerged from the basement of Washington General. *Would the Board of Directors even understand?* He took a sip of his now lukewarm coffee, tossed it in the trash can, and punched the up button for the elevator. *Even Starbucks tastes bad when it's cold.* He heaved a sigh and leaned against the wall, just as Paul Gallo came around the corner.

"I thought you had a meeting," he said, stopping.

David nodded. "I still have ten minutes, I'm using every one of them."

"Looking forward to it, huh?"

"Like a root canal."

The elevator door opened and David got in. "See ya, Paul."

Washington Hospital Group's Board of Directors featured doctors, lawyers, important business people, and major hospital contributors from the Washington-Metropolitan area. The twelve member board had unanimously voted for the FDA trials of Reel Skin to be done in their anchor hospital, Washington General. It would be great publicity and bring in badly needed dollars by patients seeking the amazing product once it was on the market. It would mesh perfectly with their burn unit at Suburban Hospital in Bethesda, also in the "group" as the board called it.

David strode into the meeting amidst whispers and the shuffle of papers. He went right to the podium and gathered his slide equipment together for the short presentation he had planned.

David's body tensed as he addressed the board.

"Thank you all for coming. We'll have a short slide presentation, then we'll get into the specifics of Reel Skin."

The sweat beaded up on David's brow as he flipped through the slides. He sensed a bewilderment on the faces of the members as they gazed at the screen. Some of the pictures were graphic burn photos. Meant to drive home the point. *This was these patients' last hope!*

One of the slides drew a gasp from a female board member and she threw her hand over her mouth then got up and walked out. When he finished, perspiration covered his upper lip and brow. Finally, after calming himself, he flipped on the lights and closed his notes. After a final question and answer session, he closed by thanking everyone and pledging to make Washington General; a state of the art burn center.

As the board members filed out, David noticed several members who were still clown-white from the troubling photo slides. *They have no idea.*

David was heading out the door when Jeffery Vorell stopped him.

"Dr. Reel, could I possibly see you in my office for a few minutes?"

David exhaled silently. "Sure, I'll meet you there."

Chapter Twenty Four

Jeffery Vorrell's office was a plush administrative suite on the fourth floor with a massive mahogany desk and expensive Oku lithographs. David had rarely visited there, and now, he wondered why this urgent meeting was necessary.

Vorrell greeted David politely at the door and showed him in. Behind his huge desk he looked even smaller than he really was. After he settled into his chair and cleared his throat a few times, his smile vanished.

"You look tired, Dr. Reel."

"I am...a little."

Vorrell furrowed his brow. " A little? I told you before, we can postpone these meetings if we need to. I know how hard you work."

"It's not the work, I've just been under a little strain, that's all."

Vorrell stood from his desk.

"I'll be frank with you, Dr. Reel. The board is worried about you. You are under a *lot* of strain, for whatever reason. You know it and I know it. Around here everyone knows it. It's the talk of the hospital."

"I thought the meeting went pretty well," David countered.

"What there was of it. I understand the tremendous pressure you must be under. This is a monumental discovery you're about to unveil. But this goes beyond that. You're not yourself. You're *detached.*"

David shifted uneasily. "I'm sorry. It's something I have to work out."

"Maybe you shouldn't try by yourself. I won't pry into your private life, it's none of my business. But if things don't change, the board is going to have second thoughts about your funding."

David fell silent.

"And that's not a threat, Dr. Reel. It's a fact. We need this as much as you do, but people's lives are at stake here. I can't have one of our top surgeons falling to pieces during a surgical procedure. Don't ruin this now."

"I'm fine."

Vorrell sat on the edge of his desk. "Very well, but if you make a fool of yourself, don't say I didn't warn you."

A murky silence fell over the room.

David couldn't get out of Vorrell's office fast enough. It was true. He was a mess right now. But Vorrell only saw one side of the equation. The whole picture was far more complicated than his narrow mind could ever imagine. David just needed a little more time.

Then he would make everything right.

Chapter Twenty Five

Mr. Henry's Pub was packed and lively, the Georgetown crowd jammed shoulder to shoulder, three-deep at the bar. Cigarette smoke was thick, and the music blared from speakers everywhere. The room was dark, the crowd was dressed up, and the place was too loud to hear anything Paul Gallo wanted to say. David had invited Paul to share some pizza and a few beers, but now he wondered if it was a good idea after all.

Paul ordered and the beers came and the two men held up their mugs in a mock toast.

"So what happened with Vorrell?" Paul asked.

"Not much. He's concerned."

"He's concerned about his ass, is what he's concerned about."

David nodded "I know. But I'll play along."

Paul leaned back. The two of them sat their mugs down on the scarred table and looked out at the crowd. Mr. Henry's was in its glory, the weekend had begun. People drifted in from Wisconsin Avenue, still dressed in their business suits. Many political power brokers from D.C. David felt out of place.

He leaned forward, set his beer down and looked Paul in the eye.

"Vorrell thinks I'm losing it," he said. "What do you think, Paul? Am I losing it?"

"No, I don't think I'd go that far. You might need to slow a little after these trial surgeries, but I don't think you're ready for a straight jacket."

David smiled. "That makes me feel better."

"There is one thing though, David. You need to let the past go. Get on with your life. You can't bring them back."

David was stunned. Paul's words were prophetic.

Chapter Twenty Six

David arrived at the lab the next morning early enough to watch the sun rise, spreading a fiery orange glow over the crisp lawns and gridlike streets of Rockville. He wished he had done this more often. Watching the city slowly awaking, as he arrived rather than when he was leaving. It made him think of the ways in which things might have been different.

Inside the lab, it surprised David to see Jean Stokes already glued to her microscope.

She straightened her back. "David, you're here. How was the meeting yesterday?"

"I thought it went pretty well until the administrator invited me to a *private* meeting. He said I seemed, 'detached'."

"Detached? Don't they realize you're about to make medical history? That's enough to make anyone a little nervous. Besides, those people don't think on the same wave length as we do. They don't understand the science of it. They're only concerned with dollar signs."

"That's the truth. You should have seen how pale some of them got when I showed my slides."

Jean's eyes hardened.

"Did I say something wrong?" David asked. "No of course not. Hey, let me show you the latest batch of skin."

David felt a sudden coldness from Jean. He didn't know what he'd said to set her off, but something did. Also, that sense of familiarity returned. *Something in the eyes.*

"Now, about that skin?" he asked.

"I'm harvesting the last batch from yesterday. I was just checking samples from one of the trays."

"How does everything look?"

"Great. I think we're ready for the close-up Mr. DeMille." Jean's mood lightened.

David smiled at the obscure reference.

Maybe he had misinterpreted her? She was right about one thing. If all went as planned, the patients would have their close-up. On every medical journal in existence. Reel Skin would become the hottest product since antibiotic.

It never occurred to David to look at the slides Jean Stokes had in the microscope.

Chapter Twenty Seven

The phone call came as an unpleasant surprise. David sat the receiver on his desk, then peeked out of his office before gently closing the door.

He picked the phone back up and settled into his chair. "I thought our business was finished," he said.

"Sometimes things change. So here's the deal. I need another ten thousand to keep my mouth shut. Otherwise I might have to go to the cops and expose you for what you really are."

"And just *what* is it you think I am?"

"Hey Doc, only you have the answer to that. Whatever it is though, I'm sure they wouldn't understand your little project."

David didn't mind paying Don Spence for his services the first time. He'd gotten David what he needed. But this...this was extortion. Spence was right about one thing. No one would understand the depth of what went on in the back of the lab at night.

"How do I know you won't keep coming back?" David asked.

"As soon as you pay me, I'm leaving the country. You'll just have to take my word."

David almost laughed. *His word!*

"Hey doc, let me break it down for you again. Either you have the money by tomorrow or I go to the cops."

"Then you'll implicate yourself. And what about your partner."

"Not to worry. I've already taken care of him."

"I'll see what I can do," David finally relented.

David hung up the phone and heard a distinct click. Someone was on the extension in the lab!

Chapter Twenty Eight

David's eyes blinked open to the hum of lab equipment. It was 4:00 A.M., and the centrifuge had spun so long it literally welded the contents of the tubes to the sides of them. He straightened up from the lab table. His arm tingled from sleeping on it and he shook it vigorously to get the circulation going. The nights without sleep had wreaked havoc on his biological clock. Although his watch said it was early morning, his body insisted it was the middle of the night. He turned off the centrifuge and watched it stop as if it had air brakes. He took the tubes out and tossed them into a red trash bin marked CONTAMINATED WASTE. He'd have to run a new sample tomorrow.

Now, prepared to leave, David slipped off his lab coat and hung it on the rack next to Jean's. As he turned to leave, he noticed some black smudges on her collar along the back. Curious, he took a closer look. A distinct odor hit him the minute he pulled the jacket toward him. He took a whiff and smiled. "Women."

He knew that smell: hair dye. As unmistakable to him as the odor of the operating room. His own mother had dyed her hair frequently, and as with everything else concerning her, it was as fresh in his mind as if it were yesterday.

So Jean's raven-black hair was the product of a bottle. It surprised him since she seemed to have such natural beauty. *What did her real hair color hide?* David stepped out into the early morning mist with renewed curiosity about Jean Stokes.

Chapter Twenty Nine

"I don't understand it, Jean. He was fine when I saw him last night."

After morning rounds at the hospital, David returned to the lab. Now, there was a new problem.

"I don't know. He was like this when I came in this morning," Jean Stokes said.

David sighed. "This is disturbing. First the mice, now Dexter. Maybe we should send some cultures for pathology?"

"I don't know, with the FDA trials just days away, do you really want the hospital running cultures? You'd have to report it. Besides, I can run some cultures right here and isolate anything that might be growing."

"That's right! I keep forgetting about your microbiology expertise."

"I'll get on it right away."

Two days earlier, Dexter, David's lab monkey, had come down with a fever. At the time, David passed it off as a cold and gave him some antiviral medication, which initially got rid of the fever.

Now, however, he showed other symptoms. Things David saw as very ominous. He was lethargic, and his skin was blotchy. Several spots had opened up and now began to ooze a green purulent drainage. David suspected Dexter had been cross contaminated from the mice. Six of them had died unexpectedly the day before. The symptoms were similar. Confident Jean would get to the bottom of it quickly, David felt relieved for the moment. When he looked at Dexter though, his relief faded. The usually active simian, who had been the cornerstone of much of David's success, was now a picture of torment.

70

It saddened David to see him like this, he had a fondness for him that extended beyond the lab. Almost a pet-owner relationship. In fact once the human trials were over, David had planed on donating Dexter to the Washington Zoo. He doubted that would happen now.

Having come this far, David knew Jean Stokes had a valid point. The last people who needed know about this was the FDA. David felt certain the animal's sickness wouldn't affect his trial surgeries. The FDA, however, in its sometimes overzealous effort to protect the public, might not see it the same way.

There was a long silence. David breathed deeply as if to absorb the frightening truth. "If we don't get to the bottom of this," he said, "lab animals will be the least of our worries."

Chapter Thirty

Jean Stokes locked up the lab and wandered back to her motel, two blocks away. Once inside the dank room, she pulled the shades against the glaring headlights of passing cars. She stood before the dresser mirror, and stared at her reflection. Her brother wouldn't recognize her now. But if he did–he would see through her emotional hardness to the little girl who had been his biggest fan. He would understand her pain. It was this notion that had kept her going since his death.

Things were going well until someone named Don threatened to interfere with her plan. She would have to act on behalf of David Reel. When she listened on the lab extension, she figured out Spence was trying to shake David Reel down. She couldn't risk someone screwing things up.

Jean Stokes sat on the bed and called the number. He sounded surprised when he heard a woman's voice.

"Hello," Jean Stokes said.

"And just who is this?" Don Spence asked.

"I'm a representative of Dr. Reel."

"Would that be, as in money?"

"Yes, it would. I'd like to meet with you to drop it off."

"Why doesn't doc just do it himself?"

"He's much too busy with his work."

"I just bet he is," Spence said.

"Well, when can we meet?" Jean Stokes asked.

"You sound anxious, sugar. You aren't scared are you? Or has the good doctor told you all kinds of bad things about me?"

"No, I'm not scared. I'd just like to get this over with."

"All right. Are you familiar with DuPont Park?"

"Sure, I know where that is."

"I'll be next to the pavilion. Be there Wednesday night at nine o'clock. I'll be in a dark-blue Chevy van. And don't be late."

He hung up before Jean Stokes could say anything else. He didn't intimidate her. She'd use everything nature had given her.

Don Spence would have a night he would never forget.

Chapter Thirty One

Before heading back to work on Tuesday morning, David Reel stopped in his old neighborhood. It hadn't changed all that much except for a little more ethnic diversity, otherwise, it still looked the same. David pulled the car over and parked.

Dreary eyed, he climbed out and pulled up the hood of his sweatshirt and jammed his hands into his pockets. A tornado of yellowed maple leaves blew up around his ankles as he crossed the street. The houses all looked the same: standard split-level with brick front. The only distinguishable difference was the color of the shutters. One house in particular, however, more modern than the others, looked out of place. It was built ten years after the rest—*in the place where his house had burned to the ground.* Several families who were there that night still lived on the street. They were probably too old and feeble by now to remember though. A small boy played on a seesaw in the backyard. David's mind flashed to himself in that very place.

Dogs barked in the distance as David walked past. *Did the little boy had any idea what had happened there so many years before?*

A memory of old friends filled his mind–playing baseball together in the street, then running to the candy store. Then his thoughts turned to Sam:

They were having trouble sleeping that night. Sam had pestered David to get one of his mom's cigarettes for him.

"You don't need to smoke, Sam," David said. "Besides, if my mom wakes up, she'll brain us."

"It will be my last one I promise."

"All right, but this is the last time."

74

David went to the kitchen counter and took a cigarette and gave it to Sam, then stood guard while Sam sat on the window ledge and blew smoke rings out into the dark.

"Hurry up," David told him.

"I need my soda from the kitchen."

Sam came back from the kitchen and looked at David.

"What did you do with my smoke?"

"I didn't do anything with it."

Sam frowned. "It was right here on the window."

"Maybe the wind blew it outside."

"Yea, I guess so."

Sam emptied his soda in one big gulp and closed the window. Then they went back to David's room.

That was the last night of Sam's life. Years later after he'd obtained the Fire Marshall's report, he would learn the truth. The cigarette had not rolled out the window at all. Instead, it had fallen into the small wastepaper basket under it, where it smoldered for several hours before it catalyzed the inferno that killed Sam and ruined David's mother. He never blamed Sam. He loved him too much and only blamed himself.

David looked up to the sky. "Well, Sam," he whispered. "It won't be long."

He paused at his car to take one last look at the houses.

A car passed and jarred him out of his dream-like state. He only got a passing glace at the driver, but...*It couldn't be!*

Chapter Thirty Two

Eight surgical suites filled the entire space of Washington General's sixth floor. Suite was a term loosely applied by the board to impress JCHO inspectors, who came once a year to decide if the hospital met their "Standards of Excellence."

To David Reel, however, inspectors were a mere, self-important pain in the ass. In reality, the suites were still just plain ole operating rooms. Each room consisted of a main operating theater, with its giant kettle-drum-light in the center, a scrub room, and a small auxiliary room for reading x-ray films or preparing specimens for the lab.

Even at seven o'clock in the morning, all eight OR rooms were usually a beehive of activity. Today was no different. Except in OR number four: David Reel hoped to make history in the field of reconstructive surgery.

Norah Rhodes, the first human trial patient for Reel Skin, lay on the operating table.

On the other side of the scrub room window, David gazed out at the steady drip of her intravenous fluid while he finished the sterile wash of his hands. He realized he was going slower today than usual. Part out of fatigue, part out of anxiety. The hum of equipment generators sounded oddly ominous today. His nights in the lab were taking a toll on him, but he would soon finish that part of his work as well.

He stepped through the OR door and paused to let his vision adjust to the bright light. The air was cool and light and mixed with the potpourri of distinct smells that accompany humans in the operating room. He consulted with the anesthesiologist who was busy adjusting the parameters on the heart monitor. It traced a steady blip across the screen.

Finally, he went down the last minute checklist making sure he hadn't overlooked anything.

Next to Norah Rhodes, lay a steel tray. It held the key to her future.

David was a competent surgeon. Of course, this time, he knew, it would be more than just surgical skill that would determine the outcome for Norah Rhodes. His years of research and hard work were all on the line. His discovery would make the difference. That was beyond his control, left up to the enzymes and cells. The molecular soup that would work in harmony to make Norah Rhodes a whole person again. He could see the side of her face as the bright kettle light spilled down on her. Scars, old suture lines, and wrinkles, something—from a bad nightmare. *What she must have gone through?*

The scrub nurse finished gowning David, and he stepped back as the anesthesiologist looked down at Norah and smiled. "I'm Raj," the dark-skinned Indian doctor said.

"I'll be doing your anesthesia. In a minute I'm going to give you some medicine to help you relax."

Norah nodded.

Raj had a slight British accent and a calm reassuring manner. He was really Blaskar Rajime, but everyone had called him "Raj" since he first trained at Washington General in the eighties. David frequently requested him on his cases.

Raj reached up and adjusted the drip rate on Norah's IV, then pulled a small syringe from his jacket pocket.

"You'll be getting sleepy in a minute," he said to Norah, as he pushed the needle into the rubber port of her IV line. No sooner had he said it, than Norah's heart rate dropped on the monitor and she relaxed. David nodded at Raj.

"Okay," Raj said. "Now I'm going to give you the good stuff." He gave the signal to his assistant sitting behind the head of Norah's OR bed.

As the nurse anesthetist pushed the Pentothal into her IV line, Norah fell into a deep sleep. It was as far into unconsciousness as one could go without actually dying.

David looked up at the clock. It was 9:00 A.M. He had to finish in two hours, or the skin wouldn't be viable.

He turned to the scrub nurse, "Knife."

Chapter Thirty Three

Inside OR 4, David removed the first piece of damaged tissue from Norah Rhodes' face. He wondered what emotional scars he was removing along with it.

At one time Norah Rhodes had everything going for her. She was beautiful, wealthy, and had achieved the American dream. She was CEO of Premir Cosmetics, a firm she started in her small garage apartment, just after college. Soon, it was a publicly traded company worth multiple millions of dollars. She lived in the most exclusive neighborhood of Olney, Maryland, where she belonged to an exclusive country club. All this at the tender age of thirty-two.

Then—the accident.

David recalled the story Norah imparted to him at their first meeting: The rain was coming down in sheets that day, Norah told David. She was looking forward to a very important luncheon date at Mr. Henry's, an outside café on Wisconsin Avenue. That day, however, the weather would dictate everything. She pulled onto New Hampshire Avenue headed for Bethesda, where her business occupied an entire floor of one of the ritziest office buildings in town. The Washington commuters had traffic snarled up as usual with drivers busy on their cell phones and laptops as they crept along. At the beltway exit, another back-up awaited them.

Frustrated with the snails-pace of traffic, Norah made a quick left and headed down Rock Creek Parkway. It was the back-way, but it would save her a half hour of mind-numbing commute. The parkway sat nestled between woods that dropped off sharply into Rock Creek, on one side, and a storm sewer on the other. A main route before Rockville and its outlying areas exploded into a megapolis, it had become a study in patchwork road repair. Traffic though was light.

The rain began to descend in torrents, and caused some motorists to pull over and wait it out. Determined not to stop, Norah turned on her windshield wipers' full blast and kept moving. She slowed to forty-five, although the actual speed limit was half of that. That extra ten miles an hour would get her there a few minutes early. Her vision obscured by the relentless rain, she rounded a curve and failed to see the van pull out in front of her. The driver of the van instinctively accelerated to avoid a collision, which he did. Norah too, took evasive *action—unfortunately—it was the wrong maneuver.*

As the Mercedes front end collided with guard rail, the car erupted with the shriek of metal on metal. From the driver's seat, Norah watched as she careened out of control like a roller coaster that had come loose from its track. A blinding spray of sparks flew out beside her as the car flipped, then catapulted over the guard rail, tearing the fueltank from its moorings. The car bounded twice down the steep incline, then slid, crashing into Rock Creek. Gas streamed from the ruptured fuel tank directly into the driver's compartment where Norah now lay unconscious. Unable to smell the jetting gasoline that poured over her, it only took a second for the cigarette she'd lit a few minutes earlier to ignite her clothing. Flames ten feet high exploded into the air. The pelting rain did nothing to stem the gas fire that was now burning Norah Rhodes alive.

When the flames reached the gas tank, the blast hurtled the car through the air as if it were a scale model. Miraculously, Norah was blown clear of the wreckage–although it may have been more merciful had she not been. The whole event, Norah had said, took about twenty seconds. Norah Rhodes, once beautiful vivacious cosmetic's mogul, lay in a heap with only a trace of life—*burned beyond recognition.*

Three years had gone by since that terrible day. For Norah, it must have felt like a lifetime. She did recover, but after ten surgeries to improve her, she still was not pleasant to look at. She ran her company from a private boardroom, and allowed no one to see her up close except her doctors. Never going out in public, choosing to be as reclusive as humanly possible. Her closest employees never saw her except from the far end of a twenty-foot mahogany table in a darkened office. Even then, she wore a dark veil as if she were attending a funeral. It was a sad irony for a woman who spent her life peddling products to make women more beautiful.

David pulled his thoughts back to the OR and removed the last piece of scar tissue. Norah's face was now free of all skin. Had he not been a surgeon, the prospect of looking at a skinless face would be truly frightening.

As it was, it *excited* him. It was like a biology book with a transparent anatomy section: you could add or take away a layer of the body, just by turning the page.

David had turned Norah's first page. Now he needed to put back what he'd taken away. Only this time, with something decidedly better than what was there an hour ago. He promised her he could restore her beauty if she would put her total trust in him.

As he began the final step of the surgery, he hoped he could keep that promise.

Chapter Thirty Four

Dick Olson lit up a cigarette he knew he shouldn't be smoking and propped his feet on his desk. If Olson was anything, he was thorough. His attention to detail and relentless scrutiny was legendary.

His office, one of twenty at Interfax, contained reams of files with information on every sort of person imaginable. Stacked in every available corner and closing in on him by the month, they were proof that the world was indeed a very evil place. From murder to industrial espionage, to plainold-fashioned theft. He had seen it all. Sometimes though, Olson's thoroughness took him in directions that surprised even him.

Such was the case with Jean Stokes.

When Dr. David Reel contacted his agency for a simple background check, Olson expected a quick, problem-free procedure: something routine. However, it was proving to be anything but routine. After the National Crime Information Center computer check came back clean, he submitted a request to California Institute of Technology, the last known employer of Jean Stokes. Two weeks had passed, and now, there was still no word from them. When he called, a secretary politely told him they don't give out that information on the phone. Finally, he asked to speak to the Human Resources department about his request. They told him it was being processed–a phrase he knew from experience meant–it was at the bottom of a pile of papers somewhere, on *somebody's* desk. Olson hit one dead end after another. The woman seemed to have dropped off the face of the earth after 1990.

A credit check revealed no activity on any of her accounts, and the closure of all her bank accounts years ago. *Now she suddenly appears after ten years?* It was possible she was living overseas, but if so, it didn't appear in her application.

On a whim, Olson decided to check the Social Security Index to see if that would reveal anything about her employment history. At least he would have an amount of time employed to verify she worked there. He wanted to have something to tell Reel when he called him. Olson let out a lung shaking cough, then leaned over his computer and punched in the name and state. Five different Jean Stokes appeared on the screen. He matched the second name with the Social Security number Stokes had given. A new prompt appeared on the screen:

SEE SSI DEATH INDEX:

Olson knew the Social Security Death Index existed mainly for surviving spouses or family members who might be eligible for death benefits. It listed anyone with a Social Security number who died while gainfully employed and paying Social Security taxes, or collecting benefits.

So why was Jean Stokes name on it?

He realized that the Social Security Administration, like any big government agency, made mistakes on a regular basis. So he didn't jump to any conclusions, although he was starting to get a knot in the pit of his stomach.

After fielding a couple of phone calls and getting himself some fresh coffee, Olson turned back to his computer screen. He clicked on the menu under SSI Death Index, and the information came up:

Jean Stokes

DOB 8-19-41

DOD 4-20-90

LAST DATE OF EMPLOYMENT: 2-12-90

LAST PLACE OF EMPLOYMENT: California Institute of Technology

Los Angeles, California

Olson nearly swallowed his cigarette. Of course, it could all be one big mistake. If this information was right though, and it usually was, they buried Jean Stokes on a hill somewhere in southern California in 1990.

And whoever was working for David Reel, was anybody's guess.

Chapter Thirty Five

Inside the recovery room, David stood beside Norah Rhodes' bed and watched her blink through the eye holes of the mummy-like bandage covering her face. The only sound came from the monotonous beep of the cardiac monitor above her bed.

She raised her head off the pillow.

"Norah, can you hear me?" David asked.

She nodded yes.

"Are you in any pain?"

Norah nodded again.

David had warned her she would feel as if they had pulled her face off when she woke up. And indeed they had. In short order he had removed all the scar tissue down to the fascia and replaced it with lab-grown skin.

The surgery went smoothly, and David's initial anxiety gave way to confidence. His skilled hands removed years of torment from Norah Rhodes' ravaged face. In three days he would know if it was a success. By all indications it was. The new skin adhered perfectly. Held in place by a few steri-strips. Unheard of previously, if David was right, in seventy-two hours, Norah Rhodes would be a new woman. Reel Skin would become the standard for skin grafting.

David patted Norah on the arm. "I'm going to order some pain medicine for you. It will help you sleep. I'll be back to see you later."

David stepped across the hall from the recovery room and stopped at the nurses' station long enough to write an order for Morphine. Although he left the hospital elated, unfortunately it was short lived. He suddenly remembered what had surfaced at the lab. He postponed a meeting with the hospital administrator so he could get back and check on Dexter. He told Jean to give the animal a shot of Rocephin, a powerful antibiotic he hoped would ward off any further infection. David was still puzzled. He was meticulous about the lab animals, particularly Dexter. He was tantamount to the human trials. The DNA was so close, parallels could be drawn between success and failure with the human trials. David knew, what affected a simian, also affected a human patient. The OR, however, was a sterile environment, unlike the lab where the chance of cross-contamination between species existed. David surmised this is what had happened to Dexter.

The weather was balmy as David drove and he rolled down his window to enjoy the fresh air. Still postulating about the sick lab animals, when he passed the white brick building of the National Institute of Health, he got an idea. He could call his friend there, Dr. Harold Ross, a specialist in animal diseases. Maybe he could shed some light on the problem. But how could David approach him though, without admitting the problem lie within his own lab? Especially since he had already done his first human trial based on the results of studies in that lab. It might cause Dr. Ross to question the FDA approval if the test animals were suddenly getting sick. David rolled the window back up and decided against the idea. NIH and FDA were both government agencies who worked closely. Although David considered Ross a friend, if he thought David were trying to hide something, ethics would win out over friendship.

He and Jean would solve the problem themselves.

She was already working on it.

Chapter Thirty Six

Cindy Rudolph had been with David Reel from the beginning. A veterinary assistant by profession, she was his animal caretaker, and as so, a vital part of his research. She made sure that they cared for all the animals in the most humane way possible, while being subject to whatever experiments necessary to gather needed data. Cindy fed them, cleaned them and their cages, and provided affection all animals need. And as usually is the case. She became attached to them. Especially the larger animals like Dexter. So when he got sick, she was very upset.

He'd been fine until Jean Stokes began to work with him. Cindy wasn't especially fond of Jean to begin with. The woman came out of nowhere and suddenly seemed to have taken over the lab. Cindy understood David's need for an assistant, now that the FDA trials were under way, but Jean seemed to revel in the fact that she was the one David relied on. A position that previously fell to Cindy. Cindy could admit there was some jealously there. This, however, went further than mere female competition for the attention of their boss.

To Cindy, Jean appeared to have her own agenda, and at times acted as though she lived on another planet. Questions from staff went unanswered, she ignored phone calls, and most disturbing, she had caught Jean several times, trying to get into the back room of the lab. A room she knew to be off limits even to her. Cindy considered going to David, but knowing how much pressure he was already under, decided against it. She watched Jean though and noticed some disturbing things.

Once, over lunch, Cindy asked her about her family. Her face turned red, then she became angry and stormed out of the room. *Something about her just didn't fit.*

Yesterday, Cindy's suspicions were confirmed. After Dexter spiked a fever, Cindy gave him some Acetaminophen liquid. When she returned to his cage later to check on him, she found Jean injecting him with something, although she had no idea what. Later in the day, Dexter's skin was blotchy and blue with several boil-like lesions on his forehead.

This morning, Jean was at his cage again—only this time—*he was dead.*

Chapter Thirty Seven

Inside the lab, Cindy Rudolph caught herself pacing frantically. She wished she'd exposed Jean when she'd had the chance.

Jean Stokes sat hunched over her microscope. "You look stressed, Cindy. Something bothering you?"

"I need to talk with you."

"About what? I'm very busy," Jean said, without looking up from the microscope where she'd glued her eyes.

"About what you did to Dexter."

"What are you talking about? Dexter got an infection."

"An infection that you gave him! I took one of those petri dishes you left. I had it analyzed, Jean, I know what it is."

"You're out of your mind."

"No, I think you're the one out of her mind."

"You can't prove anything, Cindy."

"Oh I think I can. I have the lab report, and your fingerprints are all over the petri dish. And I took a sample of Dexter's blood and sent it to a friend of mine at the veterinary lab. I feel quite sure it will match whatever it is you have in that dish. I don't know what kind of game you're playing, but I'm going to call Dr. Reel right now."

"You aren't going anywhere, bitch!"

Jean grabbed the much smaller woman by her collar and jerked her around. With her free hand she fished a 15-cc syringe with a large bore needle from her lab jacket, and uncapped it.

"You should have taken the day off," Jean Stokes said, and plunged the needle into Cindy's neck. Blue fluid shot into her carotid artery, and her face went pale. Cindy Rudolph slumped to the floor and she was dying.

Jean stared down at the syringe firmly embedded in Cindy's neck as it pulsated with each final heartbeat. She reached down and calmly pulled it out. Blood sprayed up and Cindy's eyes rolled back in her head. The poison paralyzed the last of her brain cells and her hand twitched once, then her chest heaved. When her last futile attempt to breathe failed, she fell silent.

Jean recapped the syringe and placed it back in her pocket. Scarlet pools began to form on the tile floor around Cindy's head. Jean Stokes locked the front door, then hurried to the utility closet and grabbed the bucket off its wheeled-platform, filled it with hot water, and poured in half a bottle of ammonia. Choking on the fumes, she spun on her heel, and snatched a roll of paper towels from the rack and wiped up as much of the thick blood as she could. It had already started to congeal and Jean Stokes cursed it.

When she finished, she grabbed two large trash bags, she placed one over the top of Cindy's body and one over the lower half. She secured the whole thing with duct tape. With the tiny shower stall empty of its usual array of supplies, Jean dragged Cindy's body inside it and yanked the curtain closed. After reassuring herself there was no blood left on the floor, she shoved the bucket apparatus back in the closet and slammed it shut. No sooner had it banged closed, when she heard the metallic click of the front door lock. Noticing blood on her lab coat, she tore it off and tossed it in the cabinet behind her, just as David walked in.

Chapter Thirty Eight

David Reel stopped halfway across the lab and stared at Jean Stokes. "What's wrong, Jean? You look like you just ran a marathon. Why'd you have the door locked?"

"I was here by myself. It makes me a little uncomfortable. You know, me being from a big city and all."

David nodded. "That's okay. I understand. Still, you look distressed. Is everything all right?"

"Not really. I have bad news...Dexter died."

"What? Did you give him the Rocephin?"

"Yes, just like you asked, but it was too late. His breathing became labored and he developed some kind of sores on him."

"Sores?"

"Yes, sores. Yesterday they were dime size. Today they were like silver dollars. At least twenty-centimeters."

The implication of Dexter's death made David's chest suddenly feel compressed. *My God.* Had he gotten so involved in his work at night that he failed to recognize something so important occurring in his main research animal? *Had he missed something in his trial patients as well?*

"Where is he? I'd like to have a look at him."

"I put him in the lab fridge, sealed in a containment bag."

"Good thinking. We don't need anything spreading around this lab any more than it already has. Are the other animals okay?"

"So far. How'd the surgery go?" Jean asked.

"It went perfect. Of course we won't know for sure for a few days, but by all indications, it was a success."

"Great. We'll have to celebrate."

"I'm afraid I won't be able to celebrate just yet. This thing with Dexter has me worried. If it were to get out that our trial animals had died, the FDA will shut down any further work indefinitely. And by the way, where's Cindy?"

"Oh, I almost forgot. She got a call from out of town. Someone passed away, her grandmother, I think. Anyway, she said she'd be gone about a week, but she would call and let you know exactly how long when she got there."

"That's funny, I thought her only grandmother was already dead?" Jean threw up her hands. "Maybe it was an aunt, I don't know. Like I said, she'll call."

David looked around and noticed Cindy's bag she often carried with her, along with her jacket, hanging on the back of the door. "She must have left in a hurry. She left her jacket and bag."

Jean Stokes nodded. "She did. Practically ran out of here."

"All right, well I'm going to be in my office for a while, then I have to go back to the hospital and check on Norah Rhodes. If Cindy calls, have her call me here tonight. I have some questions about Dexter. I'll be working late."

Chapter Thirty Nine

DuPont Park was a favorite hangout of winos and vagrants, along with the occasional hooker trying to earn a quick buck. It was also where Don Spence conducted most of his business when he wasn't dealing drugs at the biker bar where David had met him. He had told Jean Stokes as much.

The park was mostly a grassy knoll set between large oak trees that had stood for a hundred years or more. The pavilion was an octagon brick affair off the parking lot, surrounded by a stone wall. As Jean pulled her car into the parking space, she spotted several drunks passed out along its perimeter.

She climbed out of her car and crossed the park. She walked past a wino sprawled out under a tree, hand still clutching his bottle of Night Train, unaware she was even there. She spotted the blue Chevy van on the opposite side of the pavilion. Don Spence had parked it next to an eight-foot stone wall that defined the parking area. It provided enough privacy that in the unlikely event that anyone could even focus their bloodshot eyes, they couldn't see the van.

Perfect.

"You're right on time," Spence said as Jean walked up to the driver's window.

"I'm punctual," she said in her best sensual voice. "Now are you going to invite me in or not?"

Spence grinned wide. "Sure,"

She walked around and climbed in.

"So what's your name, beautiful?"

Jean Stokes looked at the long scar on his left cheek. She touched it. "Sexy. I like a man with character."

Her first impulse was to kill him immediately. Then, she relaxed a little and decided to play along.

"My name is Cindy," she said, knowing the real Cindy no longer needed her name.

"What do you do, Cindy?" He gave her a greasy smile.

"Anything you want," she said, moving closer.

"You *are* a friendly little thing, aren't you? This wouldn't be doc's attempt to get out of paying me would it?"

He opened the console revealing a silver pistol.

She slid closer. "No, I have the money." She put her hand on his thigh. "I just want to have some fun, first."

She felt him get hard and she squeezed him there. She thought about asking him what he knew about David, but decided she didn't really care.

Spence leaned over to kiss her. His breath stunk of whiskey and decay. She turned her head.

"What's the matter?" he asked. "I thought you wanted to have fun?"

"I do…I thought I heard something."

"Nothing here but drunks. You probably heard them mumbling in their sleep."

Spence's breath assaulted her again. It smelled as rank as a dentist's rinse sink. *That's it.* She couldn't bear to wait any longer.

Jean Stokes gave him another squeeze with her left hand while she reached into her purse with her right. She retrieved a carpet knife with a retractable blade, then slid the blade out to its full length. Spence was breathing heavy and about to reach *his* full length as she moved in close beside him.

"Are you ready?" she whispered.

She jammed the carpet knife hard against his windpipe and heard a popping sound. A look of surprise burst upon his face, but all he could manage was a couple of gurgles. She sliced across and finished at the ear, and thick blood came out his neck. His head dropped back on the headrest. *Lifeless.*

Jean Stokes looked at the gaping wound. *She did not feel anything.*

She wiped the blade off on his shirt, and slipped her hand off his flaccid crotch. What had engorged it a minute earlier, now just a bright outpouring down the front of him.

Jean Stokes climbed out of the van and hurried toward her car. She paused at the wino, still unconscious from his liquid dinner. Carefully, she laid down the carpet knife on his lap. Then she took Don Spence's wallet and slipped it into the drunk's shirt pocket. It would give the police a suspect when they found Spence. They would assume Spence was just another drunk, passed out in his van.

Upon closer inspection, however, they would see—the wino had filleted him–and stole his wallet for booze money.

Chapter Forty

After a short nap in his office, David Reel headed to the hospital to check on Norah Rhodes. Ahead of him in the distance, he could see rain hanging over the Washington skyline. The gray clouds seemed to echo with the voices of distant memories. David tried to ignore them.

Forget her, he willed himself.

Denise Baker often haunted him at times like these, when he was tired or stressed. *You should be with her right now,* the voice whispered. With traffic at a standstill, he felt himself reeling backward into a time tunnel.

They met during her first-year internship at Washington General. David noticed her one day as she examined one of his post-op patients. She impressed him with her assessment skills, and at lunch, he enjoyed a lively discussion of his patient's prognosis. David knew he'd been smitten.

Not long after, David asked her out to dinner. They dined on fresh lobsters and Waldorf Salad, and chased it down with the best Cabernet the restaurant sold. David never felt so close to a woman since his mother had died. It wasn't long before Denise's clothes started to pile up at David's house. Filled with anticipation, he asked her to move in. Their first year together was loaded with passion and excitement, spending days at a time at art galleries and museums. Things David was unaccustomed to. They were as their friends observed, "inseparable."

But soon, David received his grant and the research began to eat up all of his free time. With Denise's long hours at the hospital, they soon found their relationship floundering. When they did manage to steal a few hours together, all David could talk about was his work. Soon, he became increasingly secretive and more reclusive by the day. Despite pleas from her to take a break, David became even more obsessed. Finally, she'd had enough and moved out.

Hardening his resolve, David threw himself even further into his work, spending every available minute at the lab. Eventually, the work paid off and David made his breakthrough.

Now, as traffic started to move again, it pulled David from his painful reverie. He found it ironic. Her leaving was the real key to his success. He only wished he could share it with her.

Twenty minutes later, he arrived at the hospital and hurried to the third floor. Stepping off the elevator he could see it was nothing less than organized chaos. Nurses coming on for the morning shift were getting report from the night nurses', which left call bells unanswered, leaving the patients irritated. Especially ones who needed post-op pain medication, one of which was Norah Rhodes.

When David walked into her room she banged a clipboard against her side rail. She held up the clipboard she used to communicate and pointed to what she had written. IM IN PAIN!

David glanced over at the nurse.

"Can you get her some IV Demerol, please?"

"Sure, right away," the nurse said.

Norah held up the clipboard. THANK YOU.

"You're welcome," David said.

David flipped through the temperature chart at the foot of the bed and was relieved to see she had no fever. An infection would be a catastrophe for her.

He looked down at Norah, who appeared encased in the bulky bandages.

A gruesome picture suddenly flashed through David's mind. *Norah lying in a closed casket.* Oh no!

David turned away, then looked back.

"I'll give you some additional pain medication, and something to help you rest."

Norah nodded, then her head fell back to the pillow.

David returned to the nurses' station where he pulled Norah Rhodes' chart from the carousel. He wrote new orders for Demerol 100 mg. IM, and Ambien 25 mg. po, to help her sleep. He also noticed a slight elevation in her white blood cell count, so he ordered an additional dose of IV Cipro as a precaution. He closed the chart and was about to get up when the administrator wandered up to the desk. He cleared his throat several times, then said. "Dr. Reel, how are you? I wonder if I might talk to you for a few minutes? I promise it won't take long. He cleared his throat three more times.

"Sure," David said. "Your office?"

"My office will be fine. I'll meet you there in ten minutes."

David rolled his eyes. *What now?*

Chapter Forty One

Jean Stokes wanted to throw Cindy Rudolph's body into the dumpster and let the compactor take care of the rest. However, blood running onto the parking lot tended to draw curious eyes. She needed something foolproof. And needed it fast. The body had already been hidden there overnight and David was due in this morning.

After exhausting her options, an idea occurred to her. A crematorium sign stood at the entrance to the industrial complex. She could almost see it from the lab's front window. It was one of those no frills, get your ashes back in a cardboard box places, a cheap alternative to a traditional funeral. She couldn't remember the name, but she could see the dominating sign out front in the parking lot. She stepped out the front door of the lab and walked toward the front of the complex. Not far ahead, she saw the bright green sign with bold yellow letters: CRAMER'S CREMATORIUM.

Back in and with the phone book in front of her, she dialed the number.

"Cramer's," a voice answered.

"Yes, this is Dr. Stokes from the veterinary clinic. I was wondering if you cremate animals?"

"Yes ma'am, we sure do. We have a separate furnace for them. What kind of animal you got?"

"Well it's a large monkey actually. We used it for research, but it died today. How soon could you cremate it?"

"When can you get it here?"

"I'm not far away. Say about fifteen minutes?"

"Well, I was going to lunch. I suppose I could wait a little while. You know where we're at?"

"Yes. In the Randolph Industrial Park, right?"

"That's right. And it'll be a hundred and fifty dollars, cash or check. Payable when you bring the animal."

"That's fine. I'll see you in fifteen minutes."

Jean Stokes yanked Cindy Rudolph's body from the shower stall and dragged her to the front door. Moving as quickly as she could, she pulled her car around then popped the trunk lid. With one last glance around, she hoisted the stiff corpse into the trunk and rolled it in. She locked the door to the lab, then drove across the lot to the crematorium. Before opening the door and getting out, she surveyed carefully around the parking lot to be sure she wasn't observed. She decided she was unseen.

The building was identical to the one she worked in. The crematorium was situated between two empty office spaces. *No wonder they're empty.* Working next to a crematorium would take a little getting used to. *Even for a pyromaniac like herself.*

She knocked on the door and several minutes passed. Finally, a gaunt, Icabod Crane lookalike opened the door.

"Hi, I'm Les. You the one with the monkey?"

Jean Stokes smiled. "That's me. He's in the trunk."

"All right, let me get the cart."

Les disappeared inside, while she waited. A minute later, he returned pushing a metal gurney, the kind used in morgues. Dark crimson stains covered it as though someone had thrown paint on it. *It wasn't paint.*

Les looked at her. "Don't worry. A little blood can't hurt the dead. Specially a damn monkey." He flashed a rotten-tooth smile.

Jean Stokes opened the trunk and Les looked in. "Pretty good size monkey, I'd say."

"Yes, it was an Orangutan."

"Can I have a look?" he asked.

"I wouldn't. He died under suspicious circumstances. I'd get him cremated as quickly as possible if I were you."

Les's pyorreaic grin suddenly changed to a look of concern. "I ain't gonna catch nothing am I?" he asked, pointing a nicotine-stained finger at Jean.

"Like I said, I'd get it done soon."

Les reached into the trunk and hauled out the makeshift body-bag. Jean Stokes helped him lift it onto the gurney. "I'll get him in there right now," he said, with a renewed sense of urgency.

"Good idea," Jean Stokes said. *This poor buffoon doesn't have a clue.*

She followed him as he whisked past her and into the cremation room where two doors divided it. On the right, the door read: FURNACE #1. On the left: FURNACE # 2.

Les opened the door to furnace room number two.

A slight acrid odor wafted from beyond the door. It wasn't entirely unpleasant to Jean Stokes. Just distinct. *In fact, it wasn't the first time the odor of burnt flesh had passed through her nostrils.*

The furnace stood directly in front of them, a large cast-iron affair that resembled a giant pizza oven.

"Mind if I watch?" she asked.

"Suit yourself," Les said, donning a big pair of asbestos coated gloves. He placed some oversize goggles on, the band so tight it made his ears stick out like the ears of a hyena.

He opened the furnace door and a wave of heat washed over the room. He slid the metal tray from inside, then hoisted the body-bag onto it. Les gave the tray a quick shove and it sounded like a roller coaster track pulling its cars as it disappeared inside of the huge furnace. He shut the door and stepped back, then reached up and pushed a button on the front panel. Jean could hear a rushing sound, as if someone had poured gasoline on a lit fire.

Les's grin returned. "That monkey is toast now."

"That quick, huh?"

"When I hit that button there," he said, pointing to the front of the furnace, "it shoots the temperature up to twenty-four-hundred degrees. Big time barbecue!"

If Les knew who he was talking to, he would have realized the terminology he used was part of her own vocabulary. She was quite familiar with the many aspects of fire.

"Can I pay you now?" Jean Stokes asked.

"Sure, let's go in the office. You need a receipt?"

"No. In fact, here is two-hundred dollars for a job well done." She handed him two crisp one-hundred dollar bills.

He pocketed the cash. "Now that's what I call good business....One more thing though."

Jean Stokes looked up.

"What shall I do with the ashes?" he asked.

"Just throw them away."

Chapter Forty Two

Inside Chip Conroy's hospital room that evening, David found his patient staring out the window to the grounds below. Chip looked away, finding comfort in the shadow of the draperies.

David stood a long moment and thought about Chip. After having spent six months in the severe burn unit of Chester Medical Center outside Philadelphia, after seven surgeries to reconstruct what was left of his face and neck, there was little anyone did to make him look or feel any better. Until now. His surgeon arranged for him to meet with David and sign up as a trial patient for Reel Skin. After that initial meeting, it was finally time. Once a handsome man with a thick mane of blond hair, now, Chip was not easy to look at—even for David. Maybe, especially for David. He had an empathy for burn victims that went beyond mere medical reasoning. David was jarred out of his thoughts by Chip's voice.

"Hi, Doctor Reel."

When he spoke, it was as if they had laid him out in the sun to dry; his lips looked permanently parched and raisin-like. He also bore the scars of the usual graft problems: too tight skin, scars that overlapped forming keloids, and a general look of a face that was pieced back together little by little.

David smiled "Are you ready, Chip? Tomorrow's the big day."

"I don't know. It's been such a battle."

"I promise you, this will be the last graft you'll ever need to have."

"I was just thinking…I've got nothing to lose. Except this ugly face."

"Just remember, like the song says: *Beauty is Only Skin Deep.*"

"Then why all the fuss?"

"Because you deserve to have a normal life. And I don't want your children to hurt."

"I hope you're right."

David knew he was right. Especially about his children. He knew first hand what it felt like to have a disfigured parent. Someone who didn't want to go in public for fear of ridicule. Not having a parent at school plays or Little League games. Yes, David knew the pain, *all too well*. David first read about Chip in the regional section of the Washington Post. Chip was a crop duster pilot in Delaware, and a darn good one. A decorated Viet Nam veteran, he could fly a washing machine if he had to. One afternoon after dusting a local farm, he was headed back to the small airfield he operated from. Not far from the landing strip a flock of Starlings got caught up in his propeller. The plane stalled, clipped the top of some trees, then caught fire before he could get out. His heavy flight suit kept his torso protected, but his face and neck burned down to the muscle.

He lay in intensive care for three months, while his wife and three children prayed. Without an income, his family suffered. The local Boy Scouts put on a fund raiser and announced it in the papers. That's when David had seen the article and knew he had to help. After his first meeting with Chip Conroy, he knew the man wasn't far from the edge. That fine line David's own mother had walked for so long until it was too much to bear.

"Chip, I need to take some measurements so I can complete your graft preparation."

Chip nodded. "Sure. I guess you'll need these off," he said, as he unclipped the tiny wires that held his prosthetic ears in place. Next, he removed his blond wig and sat it on the bed.

David could see the total devastation Chip had suffered through. His hair and ears were gone; without them, he looked alien. David sensed he felt that way as well.

"Chip, I know you feel self conscious, but please understand. I know what you're going through. Fire disfigured my own mother. When I see someone else that way, I only see the person behind the face. You're a good man. And we're going to make this work for you."

David took out a small tape measure and stretched it across Chip's forehead. He picked up the chart and jotted down some numbers. "Okay, that's it. All done."

"That was quick," Chip said.

"All there is to it. Now get some rest, and I'll see you first thing tomorrow."

David picked up the chart and stuck it under his arm. He shook Chip's hand before he left, and noticed a tear on his cheek. He also noticed a couple tears of his own.

Chapter Forty Three

David Reel's eyes blinked open with momentary confusion. He sat up and looked around, his senses dulled by fatigue. A moment later, red eyed and wrinkled, he realized he had fallen asleep in the lab again. It was 5:00 A.M., just enough time to get home, shower, and get back to the hospital and direct the set-up of the OR for Chip Conroy's surgery.

David looked in the incubators at the sheets of skin laid out on the antimicrobial trays. Jean Stokes was doing a great job for him, doubling production since she started. He began to trust her enough that he even considered confiding in her about the OFF LIMITS section of the lab. She never asked about it, but David knew she must wonder what he did in there all hours of the night. Still, he couldn't bring himself to tell her. No one could ever know until the time was right. David struggled to concentrate. *He felt as though his mind were going to come unhinged lately.*

He looked back at the skin trays. The expanse of deserted work area felt like a ghost town, the entire lab taking on an almost sepulchral feel. A chill seemed to have settled inside and David buttoned his lab coat.

Refocusing his concentration, he grabbed the two trays for Chip Conroy. David would carry those to the hospital himself. He couldn't risk contamination by someone's carelessness. He picked up the titanium-lined cooler and selected two trays designated: CHIP CONROY. David marked each with Conroy's name and social security number.

That left three trays. Jean would have to start another batch today.

He had used three trays last night. In addition to what his trial patients needed, he'd require a *lot more* at the lab before he was finished.

He'd have to step up production. Tonight more than ever, he would need those extra trays.

Chapter Forty Four

When Dick Olson finally got a live voice on David Reel's phone, he was as much surprised as relieved. Although he rarely started at this hour of the morning, he was becoming increasingly anxious for David Reel's safety. He had left messages for three days, when this time, a soft female voice answered.

"No, Dr. Reel is not in right now. Can I take a message?"

"Yes, this is Dick Olson at Interfax Security. Could you ask him to call me as soon as he gets in? Please tell him it's urgent."

"Yes, I certainly will."

Olson was anxious to meet with Reel. After what he'd found out about Jean Stokes, it was imperative, Reel know the truth. He figured medical espionage was the most likely explanation. Since Reel's new product was potentially worth millions, it was a prime target for a shady competitor. *Someone was trying to infiltrate Reel's lab.* How they got Jean Stokes's name was still a mystery. Maybe it was because she was highly qualified, and, well, dead? They probably figured they couldn't trace her easily. Surprise. Whoever they were, they had met their match in Olson.

He knew Reel would be disappointed. He had confided in Olson how much he was in need of this woman's services. But that point was moot now, since the woman in question was a fraud. Well at least Olson had something to tell Reel after two weeks of nothing. Better Reel found out before he hired her. Then they might steal his whole patent, or worse. Olson had seen any number of bad things happen during his career…he had no intention of letting anything happen this time.

Chapter Forty Five

Jean Stokes hung up the phone and gritted her teeth so tight they could have shattered. She kicked the trash can and swore in the empty lab.

"Godammit, why don't people stop messing with me!?"

Her voice caused the lab animals to scurry around in their cages. She slammed the door to the animal room.

She knew from snooping in David's office, this guy Olson was the one doing her employment background check. *It was urgent, he'd said. He knew something.* She could feel it. He might ruin everything.

Jean Stokes snatched the phone book from the desk and looked up Interfax Security. She dialed the number, hoping someone would pick up.

"Interfax Security," a voice said.

"Yes, Dick Olson please."

"Just a minute. Let me see if he's left yet."

Several advertisements played until it was picked up. "This is Dick Olson."

"Mr. Olson, this is Mary at Dr. Reel's lab. I gave him your message, and he wanted me to ask if it would be too much trouble for you to meet him here? He's tied up at the hospital right now, but when he's finished, he wants to see you in person."

"Well...I guess so. What time?"

"In about an hour...if that's all right?"

"Sure, I just need some directions."

Jean Stokes gave Olson the directions, then hung up.

Her ruse had worked!

She knew David wouldn't be back until late tonight. He was, in fact, on his way to the hospital to do the Chip Conroy surgery at this very minute.

Exhilarated, she went directly to the cabinet in the corner, unlocked it, and took out the strongest acid solution she could find.

Olson would be there in an hour.

Chapter Forty Six

Holland Carter knew police departments hate to share information with other departments out of their jurisdiction. Perhaps it was some unwritten law, or maybe just plain old competition to solve the case? Carter understood this, but to the average person it would seem absurd. After all, isn't the object to catch the bad guy at any cost? Apparently not.

When Carter contacted the D.C. police homicide division about the escaped psychopath, and a possible connection to a recent murder there, they made it clear: butt out. Carter had expected no less. In fact, he was guilty of it himself occasionally, and this time to a lesser degree he'd done the same thing by not telling them what *he* knew.

Lucky for him, what he did have was an informant who traveled between Washington and Baltimore and always knew the word on the street.

Carter met him at the Double T Diner, a crowded ham and egg place outside Baltimore. They slid into a booth and picked up the menu. After they ordered, Carter pulled out a manilla envelope and took out some photos.

"You know him?" Carter asked. He slid a picture across the table.

The informant took the eight by eleven and looked at it. "*Jesus Christ*, what happened to him? And no, I don't."

"I'd say he got his come uppence," Carter said.

"Who is it?"

Carter leaned back. "Donald Spence."

The informant looked slapped. "That's, Spence? I couldn't tell."

"Well the picture doesn't do him justice."

"Looks like an anatomy class."

"Any idea who might have done it?" Carter asked.

"None. That guy's been penciled in a long time for a sudden visit from the Angel of Death."

Eggs and toast arrived and Carter tucked away the picture. The informant drank coffee while Carter ate for a few minutes. Then...

"Sure you don't want something?" Carter asked.

He looked at his reflection in the napkin dispenser. "Nah., too early."

"All right. See what you can find out. There's this doctor out in Rockville. Runs some kind of lab. Spence had the guy's card in his wallet."

"Some connection?"

"Maybe, who knows?"

Carter mopped his plate with a piece of toast.

Unfortunately, he was no closer to finding the girl.

Chapter Forty Seven

Dick Olson lit up a cigarette and paced impatiently outside David Reel's lab. Surprised to find it quiet, he knocked several times and rang a courtesy buzzer next to the door, but no one answered. He expected David Reel to be there waiting for him after just talking to his secretary an hour earlier. Olson considered leaving, but felt what he had to tell Reel was too important, so he decided to let himself in. The only sound was the dull hum of a generator somewhere nearby.

Perhaps they're busy and can't hear me?

Cautiously he cracked the door and peered in at the lab's expansive interior. "Dr. Reel…anybody here. Hello."

Tossing his cigarette out, he released the door and stepped inside. Olson felt like he'd just entered a fantasy land. He'd never been in a lab before and the sight of it amazed him. Strange metal cannisters, and an array of lab glassware, lined the walls and occupied the maze of counters and tables. The blinds were pulled tight and blocked out any light from outside. A shimmering expanse of polished black tile that shone with an eerie luster gave him the unsettling sensation that the floor was transparent.

The sound of shuffling feet turned Olson's head. The noise ended as abruptly as it had begun. Then there was a silence.

An instant later, as if choreographed for some B horror movie, the lights in the lab dimmed. Then they flickered and went out. Dick Olson found himself standing in total darkness.

Chapter Forty Eight

Jean Stokes found the light switch she was looking for. She grabbed the beaker from the counter and crept up behind Dick Olson. In one swift move, she swung around and doused his head in the caustic solution.

When she looked down, Olson was on his back on the floor, holding his face and screaming. She killed the lights again and ran toward the back of the lab.

Chapter Forty Nine

With the cloud cover over the Washington area, daylight had taken a holiday and traffic slowed to a snail's pace along the section of the Beltway traffic reporters affectionately called the "Rock Creek Roller Coaster."

David Reel tapped his fingers on the steering wheel, cursing the fog first, then the melee. He had already been in the mess for an hour. David had a long day ahead of him with the Chip Conroy surgery occupying his entire day. He didn't have time nor patience to sit in traffic. Traffic aside, he had stayed late at the lab again, which was draining him physically as well as emotionally. He didn't even have time to check his phone messages. He figured Cindy probably called to explain her sudden exodus, which he still found odd. It was so unlike her to leave without calling, even in an emergency.

The traffic started to move, and David began a mental review of his second trial patient. Chip Conroy was going to be the most difficult surgery he'd ever done.

"Just stay focused," he kept repeating.

Chapter Fifty

Dick Olson felt as if he had walked face-first into a blow torch. He rolled over on the floor and squinted through bleary vision at the girl standing over him. Olson tried to pull himself to his feet but he could not. He was blinded by red-hot fire. *Help me please!*

He tried to call out, but there was no air in his lungs, only a sickening pain. "Please!" He coughed. The sound was lost on his lips. Olson tried to call out again, but his throat was searing.

The girl started to walk away toward the back door. Olson struggled to his feet, gasping for breath. He stumbled after her as she dashed into the first room she came to. Ten feet back, Olson was staggering blindly toward her.

"Please" He gasped. *"Help!"*

The girl slammed the door shut and vanished. Olson fixed his bleary vision on the door and felt his legs starting to give under him.

Suddenly the door burst open and the girl returned carrying something in her hands. A second later, Olson felt white-hot needles again shoot through the back of his eye sockets. He wailed as he hit the floor. His vision disappeared and he felt the flesh on his face sizzling.

* * *

Standing over Dick Olson once again, Jean Stokes watched as he writhed in agony in the final throes of death. When the second splash of muriatic acid finally ate through the last layers of his larynx, he stopped thrashing and lay still. She placed the beaker on the counter and walked away.

Now she had bigger fish to fry.

Chapter Fifty One

On the fourth floor of Washington General Hospital, Chip Conroy lay in his bed touching his leathery face for what he hoped would be the last time. It was 9:00 a.m. and today was the day he'd been waiting on. Dr. Reel had promised him not only a new face, but along with that face, a new lease on life.

Chip never thought he would go through another surgery, and he wouldn't have if it weren't for the empathy Dr. Reel had shown. It was as if Reel could feel Chip's pain. Chip sensed a sadness behind Reel's empathy, too. He gave the impression of someone who'd seen his own share of grief. In all the time since his accident Chip had never met a doctor with as much compassion. Perhaps it came from carrying the load of his patients, or from his own life? Either way, Chip felt confident in a way he'd not experienced before. Chip's thoughts turned to his family, just as the nurse walked in.

"We need to start getting you ready for surgery, Mr. Conroy. Dr. Reel will be here in a little while."

The nurse went to the narcotics cabinet and took out his pre-op medications. "I'm gonna give you some medicine now to relax you," she said, as she drew up ten cc's of Versed, a powerful anesthetic, and injected it into his IV port.

"Just lay back and relax. You'll be asleep before you know it."

Those were the last words Chip Conroy ever heard.

Chapter Fifty Two

Inside OR number 3, David Reel was finishing his scrub for Chip Conroy's surgery when the circulating nurse stuck her head in the door. "Dr. Reel, there's a page for you."

David heaved a sigh. "Could you take it for me please, and ask them what they want?"

Always at the most inconvenient time.

He dried off and the nurse returned. She held a post-it note and read from it. "Okay, here it is. Three south called. Norah Rhodes has a temp of 101. They gave her Tylenol, and they want to know if you want anything else ordered?"

David's heart sank when he heard Norah's name. He hoped it was just stress from the surgery—not something more ominous that had caused her to spike a temp. The rate of nosicomial infections at Washington General was very low. He couldn't imagine *that* being a factor in causing her fever. Perhaps it was a urinary tract infection trying to take hold? They had removed her catheter, but it was still possible she caught something during insertion.

The nurse tapped her fingers while she waited for David to answer.

"Just tell them to get a clean catch urine for STAT analysis. I'll be up to see her after surgery."

David looked through the glass of the scrub room. He gazed at the figure of Chip Conroy lying on the operating table. Taking a deep breath, he stepped through the door.

Inside the OR, the surgical team was in place. David extended his arms before him, feeling a tug as the circulating nurse wrapped him in a surgical gown and fastened it behind him. David held out his hands for sterile surgical gloves, wrapping them around his fingers until they were a second skin.

On the steel table, Chip Conroy lay draped in blue cloth. It framed a face that could have come from a bad horror movie. At his side were two trays of surgical instruments and a sizable mound of gauze pads. David let his gaze drift the length of Conroy's body, then back to his face.

Anesthesia had him intubated and the Nitrous Oxide machine hissed quietly as it delivered Chip to a deeper place.

Gerald Lang, the anesthesiologist, checked the clock, then made a notation in his logbook. "We're prepped and ready."

"Thanks, Jerry…"

David's mind wandered to Norah Rhodes. Then he looked back at Chip and took a deep breath. The nurse's message had left him increasingly anxious about Norah. He couldn't let self-doubt cloud his judgment. Everything was done right with her. It was probably what he suspected, *just a urinary tract bug.*

Norah Rhodes would be fine, so would, Chip Conroy.

The staff around the operating table looked at David. "You okay, Dr. Reel?" the scrub nurse asked.

The operating room was a cool fifty-eight degrees, and he hoped–bacteria free. Norah Rhodes was on his mind.

"Scalpel," David said.

Chapter Fifty Three

After getting Dick Olson's body into the trunk of her car, Jean Stokes went back inside the lab. She stood over the maze of high tech equipment and mixed up the soupy contents of the test tube, then emptied it into one of the skin growth trays. She marveled at the mixture and how nature could create so perfect a reproduction of human skin from a hoge-poge of chemicals. She added the matrix as the final ingredient, then watched in amazement as the entire contents gelled into a transparent sheet. It would become skin in forty-eight hours.

David never revealed to her what the matrix consisted of. It really didn't matter. She had her own agenda.

Too bad. In another life, she would probably have liked David Reel. He had turned out better than she'd expected. Still, he had caused her unfathomable pain. Now he had to pay.

She went to her desk and pushed back some papers where she kept the perti dishes. If David knew what they contained he would have to destroy everything in the lab. She removed one of the small dishes and took it back to the skin trays. Using tiny forceps, she removed a spec of green material from the dish. She placed it in the center of the skin sheet where it disappeared into the soft soon-to-be skin. There the bacteria would grow and nourish, and by tomorrow, it would have multiplied ten-thousand fold. *Just as in the skin she had prepared for Norah Rhodes and Chip Conroy.*

And just the way she would prepare *all* the skin for David Reel.

Chapter Fifty Four

Inside OR number 3, David Reel trimmed back the surgical drape around Chip Conroy's face. How the poor guy had coped with the sight of himself was beyond David. The face looked like they had literally taken it apart, then put it together again without regard for ascetics. And in fact that is exactly what had happened. The inferno that raced through the cockpit of his plane took it apart. Then, a team of well-meaning surgeons painstakingly attempted to put it back together—piece by skin-grafted piece.

Unfortunately, though their intentions were honorable, they possessed neither the skill, nor the technology, to give Conroy's face a sense of normalcy.

David made a series of quick incisions across the top of Conroy's skull in a starlike pattern. "Scissors," he ordered.

David thought of Conroy's family as he cut away the scarred tissue from the man's forehead. They were all waiting in the lounge to see whether the operation would be a success. It brought back painful memories of his own mother, and the failure of every surgery to do little more for her than make her a more normal looking freak.

David would change that. *Or would he?* "Tilt him to the left," David ordered.

The anesthesiologist rolled his chair away from the monitors to Conroy's side. "Got it," he said. "Let's be careful though, David, his pressure is really low."

He gave David a pointed look as David cut away a sizable piece of flesh from the Conroy's neck. David knew he would have to be careful here, any slip up and Conroy's face would be paralyzed. His surgery was foolproof, yet he still had an uneasy feeling. He tried to focus as his assistant slapped a hemostat into his hand. He hesitated and cocked his head slightly. He looked carefully, much like a sculptor would do when deciding how to approach a piece of stone. He smiled at the nurse next to him, then gently made his cut.

"Careful," the anesthesiologist said. "Pressure, one-twenty over sixty five...now, one hundred."

David continued to cut. "Increase the IV fluids. I've got to get this scar tissue off."

He shifted into a state of complete concentration as he dissected the carotid and phelnic arteries from the neck muscle.

"Dammit," he said. "Got a bleeder." A red streak shot across his surgical gown. The assisting nurse jerked with a shock, jiggling the suction catheter. "Steady now," David said. He calmly inserted two clips and staunched the blood vessel.

"Irrigation," David ordered.

Anesthesia called out, "Pressure's dropping, one hundred... ninety..."

David stepped back and held his instruments in front of him. His body flushed.

"Oh shit!" the anesthesiologist said an instant later. He fumbled with his log book. "Pressure's at twenty over zero. Now there's no pressure. *I can't get him back!"*

Chapter Fifty Five

Jean Stokes stepped out of the lab and into David Reel's office. Her task was to erase the message that Dick Olson had left on David's answering machine. Luckily, David made a habit of only checking his messages on Friday. As she took the small tape from the machine, her curiosity got the better of her, so she felt compelled to snoop in the file drawers.

Ransacking his files, she hardly noticed when a manilla envelope dropped to the floor. She gave it little thought other than to remind herself to put it back. Most of the files were invoices for equipment, or receipts David needed for tax exempt status, since his lab was nonprofit and funded by a government grant. There were a couple of receipts for recent purchases of vacuum chambers; a fact she found odd, since all the skin was grown in hyperbaric oxygen chambers. There were no vacuum chambers she was aware of. She did remember two large crates delivered by Baxter Medical a couple of weeks earlier, but she'd not seen the contents. David had them moved to the back of the lab the minute they'd arrived. *She'd have to see about that.*

She bent down to pick up the envelope and the seal in the upper left hand corner caught her attention: MONTGOMERY COUNTY POLICE DEPT. FORENSICS DIVISION.

Jean Stokes opened the clip that held the envelope closed and slid her hand inside. She could feel pictures and a piece of paper on top. She pulled out the paper and read the large letters: OFFICIAL AUTOPSY PHOTOS.

She gazed at the pictures and the names written in black marker along the white border.

And the date! August 13, 1978.

The blood drained from her face and she heard the heavy thudding of her own heart. She gasp in horror at the images. The room tilted sharply under Jean Stokes.

Then blackness....

Chapter Fifty Six

Inside Washington General, David Reel descended the three flights of stairs from the OR in a preoccupied daze. Several co-workers passed him and said hello, but it was if he hadn't seen them. His head pounded. He walked into the staff lounge and peeked out the window. Foot traffic was heavy on Connecticut Avenue. Men in three-piece suits hurried to make their lunch dates, while fashionable women, window-shopped in the expensive boutiques. It was Washington's version of New York's Fifth Avenue. His own office was just a few doors down, and many of these same women were patients of his. He hoped Norah Rhodes would be back in those shops soon and be able to end her reclusive life. Things had improved slightly for her. The fever had broke and she was able to tolerate liquids.

Now David had to worry about Chip Conroy. *Had he missed something in the pre-op assessment?* The surgery was going well until Conroy's blood pressure bottomed out and he had to be coded. He still hadn't recovered from his anesthesia. His vital signs were stable though, and as Jerry Lang had told him, some patients just take longer than others. Normally that would satisfy David, except Lang was not among the best anesthesiologists at the hospital, and they both knew it. His presence had created a sense of anxiety that David certainly didn't need. He'd tried to get Raj, but he was at a seminar. David knew his next move was a critical one. He couldn't afford to have anything else go wrong. The entire future of Reel Skin was riding on these trial patients. He forced himself not to dwell on it. He already had enough distractions.

He went to the nurses' station and jotted down a few post op notes on Chip Conroy's chart, and he ordered an additional antibiotic as a precaution. He handed it to the nurse. "Let me know when he wakes up. I'll be down in the lounge."

"No problem. I imagine it's gonna be a while though. I was just in there and he's still out cold. Vitals are good though."

David nodded and headed to the doctor's lounge. If he was lucky, he could catch a couple hours sleep, make a final check on his two patients, then get back to the lab to complete what he'd started last night.

In slow motion, David descended the stairs. He decided to stop by the pathology lab to check on the cultures he'd ordered on Norah Rhodes. She had improved, but he needed to be certain of what he was dealing with.

David wasn't a frequent visitor to the Pathology department. In fact, he'd only met Chief of Pathology, Stanley Coblentz once. That was in the cafeteria line, hardly a formal introduction. Coblentz, a Burgess Meredith look-alike, with glasses as thick as the ones Meredith wore in his famous *Twilight Zone* episode, was hunched over his microscope when David walked in.

Did he even need a microscope with glasses that thick?

When Coblentz finally looked up, it almost startled David; the lenses gave his eyes a bug-like quality that was disconcerting. His grey hair wanted to go in every direction, and he obviously was a man who either didn't have the time, or didn't take the time to groom himself. David got the impression his work was his only priority. Despite this, he smiled affably at David.

"Dr. Coblentz, David Reel."

"Yes, Dr. Reel. You're getting quite popular around here. Congratulations on your discovery. It's quite amazing from what I understand."

"Well I appreciate that, but that's why I'm here. I'm a bit concerned about my first two trial patients."

Coblentz scratched his chin. "Yes, I saw you sent some cultures up earlier. What is it you're looking for exactly?"

"I'm not sure. It's just the first surgery went perfectly, yet the patient was still febrile forty-eight hours post op. Even with some heavy antibiotics. I just can't take any chances. Is there any way to speed up the culture results?"

Coblentz pondered David's question for a few moments, then adjusted his heavy glasses. "I'll do my best to give it top priority. You say the patient is still febrile?"

"Not right now, but it seems to come and go. And I just finished with the second patient, so I want to be sure it's not something in the OR."

Coblentz stopped fiddling with the slides and gave David his full attention. "I doubt that, Dr. Reel. We have the finest infection control team anywhere. There's not been a significant nosicomial infection here in several years. More than likely your patient picked up a stubborn urinary tract bug. Just the same, I'll run those cultures right away and get back to you."

David thought for a moment. Perhaps Coblentz was right. David wondered if he was just being paranoid. "Great," he finally said. "I'll call you tomorrow."

"You do that," Coblentz said, turning his attention back to his microscope.

It appeared to David that Coblentz had reached his threshold for conversation and needed to get back to his work, which was also his compulsion–a fact David understood all too well.

Chapter Fifty Seven

Jean Stokes found herself on the floor of the lab office with the room still spinning. For a few moments, her mind had stopped. She felt first pain, then numbness, as though someone had struck her a hard blow which spread to her whole body. She couldn't move, it was hard to breathe, her heart raced.

Realizing that she had fainted, the room around her had appeared far away, as though seen from the wrong end of a telescope. The numbness had increased until her limbs were led, she could feel nothing.

As she came full awake, the feeling ebbed slowly. In its place, she began to feel anger, an awful repressed anger that she couldn't control. She wanted to run, but couldn't. It was the kind of anger she'd felt as a child. An anger that came from a helplessness to control the inevitable.

When the room came into focus, Jean remembered she was in David's office. Next to her, scattered on the floor, lay the photographs from the police file. Suddenly, the wave of nausea returned, and she felt faint. She jammed the pictures back in the manilla envelope and closed it.

If Jean Stokes had possessed even a small amount of sanity before, to at least give the impression of normal when she needed to, *this was too much*. The only thing that mattered to her now was to *kill* David Reel.

She grabbed the envelope and stuffed it back in the file drawer. He would be back soon and although she was ready, she had a few more details to attend to first. She didn't want him to suspect anything by having things amiss in his office. *And Olson's body had to be disposed of.* She turned out the light and locked up, then slipped out the door.

Be patient, she told herself. To just put a bullet in him would be too easy.

Jean Stokes had a better plan.

Even if she had to fake it a little longer.

Chapter Fifty Eight

David Reel awoke amid the clutter of his desk with his pager beeping incessantly. He checked the number on the device's small screen and saw it was the hospital switchboard. He reluctantly dialed the number, a distant chill rising in him, wondering what they wanted.

"Washington General. May I help you?"

"Yes, this is Dr. Reel. Did someone page me?"

"Yes, Dr. Reel. Third floor south needs to talk to you. I'll put you through. Hold on."

David's pulse quickened. The click of the phone cut his thoughts short.

"Dr. Reel?"

"Speaking."

"It's Carol, on third south. I just wanted to let you know, Norah Rhodes' fever has subsided and she's requesting some food. I just wanted to find out what kind of diet you wanted for her?"

"That's wonderful news! Just give her anything she can drink through a straw. I'll be in there in an hour or so."

David hung up the phone and leapt to his feet. Despite having been up all night in the lab, this latest bit of good news gave him a renewed sense of energy. After all his worry, it seemed Coblentz was right. Just a nasty, urinary tract bug. The antibiotics had taken care of it, and if all went well, David could discharge Norah tomorrow. As for Chip Conroy, he was still not awake. Maybe he would improve soon as well?

Turning around, David caught his reflection in the plaque that hung behind his desk.

He'd placed it there soon after he opened his lab. A single Latin phrase, it held deep meaning for David: *"quantum mutatus ab illio."* Beneath it was the English translation:
"How changed from what he once was!"

Chapter Fifty Nine

One week after surgery, Norah Rhodes arrived at David Reel's office in the Medical Arts Pavilion. The crowd that usually filled the reception area was sparse. Norah found a measure of comfort in that. Even with her trademark veil, and with gauze covering her face, she still felt self conscious. That thought gave way to a happier one: *Today could possibly be the last day she'd have to cover her face with anything.* When they removed the two feet of bandages, she might be normal.

Norah got on the elevator with trepidation like she'd never known. She had endured three years of pure hell. Now she was about to be resurrected–*maybe?*

What if something went wrong? She couldn't bear the thought.

The third-floor bell rang and she passed two people getting on the elevator as she got off. What did she look like to them? Surely they could see the gauze beneath the veil. The veil itself was a giveaway. No one wore them anymore unless attending a funeral. It didn't matter, the decisive moment was near.

Reel's office was directly in front of the elevator and Norah walked right in, relieved there were no other patients in the waiting area. She paused in front of the reception desk as the nurse handed her the sign-in clipboard.

"Hi, Norah. Today's the big day," she said.

Norah nodded. Attempts to speak through the gauze proved more trouble than they were worth. Her words came out garbled as if she'd suffered a stroke.

"Dr. Reel is not here yet. I'm expecting him any minute."

Norah took a seat. She picked up a copy of Mademoiselle from the small table next to her and studied the model on the cover. *Would she look as natural as this girl?* Or would she just be another plastic surgery case with skin stretched too tight?

David Reel had assured her after the surgery she would look natural. She hoped he was right, but she still had her doubts. Even if she looked normal, would her contemporaries still think of her as fake. Either way, it had to be better than living in shame. *Please God, let this be right.* It seemed like hours to Norah, although it was only fifteen-minutes before the nurse called her back.

David Reel met her at the door of the exam room.

"Are you ready?"

Chapter Sixty

David opened the dressing change kit and took out the disposable scissors. He clipped a small piece of gauze from Norah Rhodes' bandage and began to unwrap it. He unwrapped with one hand, he rolled the gauze back around his other. With each successive layer removed, he felt as though each one represented a year of his work. As he got to the last layer, his pulse quickened. It would reveal the results of five-years of hard labor.

"Okay, Norah, I'm down to the last layer. I want you to remain very still."

Norah nodded.

The first hint of success he saw, was at the hairline. There, he had joined the first sheet of Reel Skin to Norah's scalp. There was no redness, *no scar–just a normal hairline.* David felt a wave of relief radiate through him. He peeled more gauze off until he reached the bridge of her nose. This was a critical point; the fire had totally erased Norah's nose. Previous attempts to rebuild it had left little more than a blurb on her face. Now, he could see that the nose he fashioned, had taken well. When a smile formed across his face, he looked into Norah's eyes and saw them light up for the first time since he'd met her.

The nurse, standing behind David put her hand over her mouth. "It's unbelievable."

Slowly, David finished unwrapping then set the gauze on the exam table. "Turn to the left," he said to Norah. "Now to the right."

The results were amazing, but he let the technical aspects dictate his thinking. "Open your mouth wide. Look up. Down. Now smile. Now Norah, recite the alphabet."

Norah began, "A, B, C, D, E"…finishing with Z, she looked at David.

"Great," David said, now he let his emotions show. *And* for just a minute, David saw his mother's face in Norah Rhodes. "Norah, we did it! Take a look."

* * *

The nurse handed Norah a mirror. She looked, but at first it was as if she were looking at a stranger. Norah hadn't seen *that* face in three years. She had almost forgotten it. Her scarred face was now completely clear. Her skin was as soft as her five-month-old niece's.

"It's so smooth, so perfect," she said, barely able to speak.

"That's the great thing about it," David said. "It's brand-new skin with no age to it. So it's like your face is not only restored, but reborn."

Norah stood up and embraced David Reel with all the sincerity she possessed. "Thank you, Dr. Reel, you've given me my life back."

"Just be happy, Norah. Live your life happily. There is one thing, though."

Norah sat forward.

"The FDA will want to review the results. I'll have to arrange an appointment here. After all, you are now the standard for skin grafting. They will want to move faster after they see you."

"Whatever you need, Dr. Reel, it's all right with me."

Norah Rhodes left the office still carrying the veiled hat. Still not quite believing what she now saw in the mirror. When she got to the trash receptacle, she tossed in the hat.

It was the most liberated she'd felt in years.

* * *

David Reel was a mixture of elation and worry. A new problem was overshadowing his success with Norah Rhodes. Jean Stokes seemed like the most reliable employee he had ever had, albeit somewhat elusive. He had called her at every spare moment for the past three days, but she was nowhere to be found.

He returned to his desk and sensed his growing irritation. Her absence was beginning to compromise his plans. David picked up the telephone and called again. After ten rings, he slammed the

receiver down. *First Cindy, now Jean.* Irritation turned to concern.
He had to find Jean Stokes.
If he didn't...
He shut his mind to that grim possibility.

Chapter Sixty One

Dick Olson had died a gruesome and painful death, even by Jean Stokes' standards. She had plucked the stopper from the muriatic acid bottle and splashed his face, not once, but twice, just to be sure, leaving it to burn through two layers of skin and into the muscles of his neck. His screams became mere gurgles as the acid seared his throat shut. With his windpipe cooked, it wasn't long before respiratory failure—led to respiratory arrest—and the end of his life.

Now, her plan for David Reel now so preoccupied her, she'd forgotten all about Olson and what to do with him, or more accurately, *what to do about his body?* She had hastily stashed him in the trunk of her car, and he had begun to decompose, leaking bodily fluids into the plastic sheet that covered him. *He stunk–badly!*

Currently in need of food, and en route to the grocery store, Jean Stokes found herself surrounded by the putrid odor of his corpse every time she came to a stop and the airflow inside the car diminished. By the time she arrived at the store, she had lost her appetite, but even murderers needed to eat, she reasoned, so she continued with her plans. She parked the car far away from other vehicles so as not to arouse suspicion. Anyone within ten feet of it would probably report it; a policeman with experience could recognize the sweet sickly odor of a rotting corpse.

Jean dismissed the thought and regained her composure as she entered the store. The smell of fresh produce replaced the odor of decay in her nostrils, and her nausea subsided. As it did, she began to formulate a plan to rid herself of Olson. She knew the store had a hardware section, so she set out intent on finding a five-gallon gas container. Suddenly her appetite returned.

It was the thought of fire.

Chapter Sixty Two

As the first scalpels of sunlight sliced through the window blind, Norah Rhodes awoke to find a stranger in her bed. She grabbed the covers in hasty retreat and pulled them close to her. A second later, as the initial start wore off, she realized what she had done. She looked across the king-size bed, and a smile formed across her face.

After years of self-induced chastity, and a libido that she'd buried for as long, Norah had brought home a lover. A popular watering hole in Georgetown had been the site where she'd gone for that explicit purpose last night. It was the first time since the accident she'd been with a man. With her new face and renewed self-confidence, she had done what she once thought she would never do again.

And it was wonderful. He was a considerate lover and she'd never felt so beautiful.

Norah laid her head back on the pillow. She couldn't believe it. Just six months earlier, she was severely depressed and was destined to live the life of a disfigured recluse. Just to go out in public required a veil to cover her ravaged face. Children would scream at the sight of her. Now she had her life back. The man in her bed was tangible proof. Yet, as she lay in bed, something troubled her. A sudden chill climbed the ladder of her spine, causing her mood to darken. Something just didn't feel right.

Perhaps, it was the fear of rejection. The rejection of both her lover, and the rejection of the skin graft that covered years of torment on her previously horrific face. It was a week after surgery, and they had told her because of the type of injury she sustained, there would

137

be days when she would experience a type of psycho-operative stress disorder. It would abate with time.

But why now?

Still uneasy and feeling foolish, Norah let out the breath she was holding and slipped from beneath the sheets. Her guest snored in post coital slumber, unaware of Norah's growing anxiety.

She caught her silhouette in the full-size mirror. It appeared jagged and ill proportioned in the semi-dark room.

Ridiculous. Yet something in her face didn't seem right: an unwelcome tingle, a menacing quality. She recognized the absurdity of her fear, but this did not diminish her anxiety. Terror courted her, and she was wrapped in the arms of panic.

In the half-bath adjacent to the bedroom, Norah switched on the light. As she stepped to the sink, sudden fright cinched her chest, and her heart felt painfully compressed. She was afraid to look in the mirror. Abruptly weak, she bent forward and gripped the pedestal sink with both hands. She gazed down at the empty bowl. Norah Rhodes was so bowed by fear that she was physically unable to look up.

The mirror waited. When she finally looked up, she stepped back and put a hand over her mouth. Her throat felt thick, suffocating. *Please go away.*

But after two minutes, they didn't go away. *Three dark blotches along the jaw line of her reconstructed face.*

Norah turned on the faucet and grabbed a washcloth from the towel rack. She soaked the cloth and rubbed vigorously at the marks. *No change!*

The marks seemed to throb with a thick slow pulse of their own. In the quiet of the bathroom, her breathing was alarmingly rapid and ragged with an unmistakable note of desperation.

Norah threw the washcloth down in the sink and stared at it. Perhaps if she didn't look for a while they would go away. The same strategy had worked for her as a child. Many nights when she would awake from a bad dream she would hide under the covers and not look until the boogeyman went away. Then it was all right.

She would have fled the room, but all her strength had drained from her. She tried to reassure herself hoping to bring some logic to it. *They were just blotches. Mere discoloration for God's sake. It didn't mean graft rejection.*

Logic didn't work. In a dark territory of her mind that she'd traveled before, Norah found only fear. She convinced herself that the graft had gone bad. Norah envisioned her face as *The Phantom of The Opera.* As it once was.

Trembling, she closed the bathroom door. She looked at the mirror again. "What's happening to me?" she asked her reflection.

With her fear boiling over, she grabbed the phone off the vanity table and mashed the autodialer for David Reel's office. When the message started, she slammed the phone down.

I need to speak to a human.

Next she dialed the hospital, and was put on hold. She couldn't wait. *Please God, don't let this happen to me.*

She looked at the mirror again, and her heart raced anew, the blotches remained. They seemed to have grown in size in the last few minutes. She leaned in closer. They began to ooze. The first signs of graft rejection.

Or worse!

Chapter Sixty Three

David Reel's heart nearly came to a stop when he took the call from Norah Rhodes. "Come to the hospital immediately. I'll arrange for a direct admission," he said.

As the implications of Norah Rhodes' phone call to David began to settle on the dazed doctor, he found himself weakened by a wave of panic. But before he could recover from that, he got a second call.

Chip Conroy's nurse called to advise him that Chip's dressing was saturated with a green foul-smelling drainage. To make matters worse, he still had not recovered from his anesthesia. David didn't want to believe what his scientific mind was telling him. At the lab the day before, he had retrieved Dexter from the makeshift morgue-refrigerator where Jean Stokes had left him. He took some scrapings from Dexter's lesions and viewed them under the microscope. He wasn't sure, but he had suspicions of what it was.

God help him if he was right!

David's mind went into overdrive.

He needed to get to the pathology lab and talk to Coblentz—*fast.*

Chapter Sixty Four

Jean Stokes barreled down County Road 281 intent on finding an out of the way place to bury Dick Olson. Two miles outside of Olney, she came to a small convenience store with a couple of gas pumps, and little else.

Perfect. No one would smell Olson.

Stokes smiled at the girl behind the register.

"Could you tell me how to get to Pine Quarry?"

"Pine Quarry," the girl repeated. "What do you want at Pine Quarry?"

"I'm just curious that's all."

The girl frowned, then took a slip of paper next to the cash register. "Okay," she said, as she drew a square on the paper. "We're here. You go down two miles to Granite Road. Turn right. You'll see an old church. Anyway, go about two miles and you'll see the sign for Pine Quarry. Got it?"

"Got it," Stokes said, admiring the girl for being brave enough to let someone put an earring through her upper lip. "And thank you."

"No problem," the girl said.

No doubt she'd gone to Pine Quarry. It was a well-known make-out spot at one time and probably still was, Jean had heard.

The quarry was ten miles outside Olney, Maryland. Largely used as a dumpsite for worn-out tires and washing machines nowadays, at one time it was once a thriving stone quarry. *It would be the perfect place to get rid of Olson's rapidly decaying body.*

Chapter Sixty Five

A look of serious concern replaced the usual affable smile on Stanley Coblentz's face. David recognized it immediately when he walked into the pathologist's office. His own angst grew as he plopped down in an over-size leather chair next to the desk. He could only imagine what the bug-eyed doctor had to tell him.

David looked around Coblentz's office. It was as sloppy as the man himself. If it weren't for his reputation as a top pathologist, David would be skeptical about anything the man told him. Anyone could mistake him for a crackpot based on first impressions. David knew better though, and as Coblentz glared down at him, he braced himself.

"Dr. Reel, I was just about to call you." He was sitting behind his massive desk.

"I was afraid you were going to say that."

"Afraid? I don't follow you, Dr. Reel. I thought you wanted me to hurry up on these cultures."

"Oh, I do, it's just now–"

Coblentz cut him off. "If you're about to tell me the problem with your patient on three south, I'm already aware of it. In fact I've already taken blood cultures."

Coblentz's tone was the next warning of what was to come. David watched as Coblentz removed his heavy glasses and placed them on the blotter.

David wondered if he could still see.

He studied Coblentz's face. His eyes appeared red as if he hadn't slept. He could just make out the web of fine capillaries spread across the tip of his nose.

"Dr. Reel. What we have here is the beginning of what could become a major catastrophe for this hospital."

David sat up in his chair. He still didn't know where the conversation was headed.

Suddenly, Coblentz bounded out of his chair and began pacing the area behind his desk. "Three weeks ago," he continued, "several cultures of Necrotizing Fasciitis, better known as 'the flesh-eating bacteria,' were stolen from the pathology lab at NIH. The only reason I knew about it was that they sent a bulletin out to pathology labs in the area to alert us." He stopped pacing and looked across at David. "You can understand the implications if this thing were to get out into the general hospital population."

David nodded in agreement, almost in a trance as Coblentz continued his lecture.

"When I ran the cultures you gave me, I was shocked to discover the same strain of bacteria. Dr. Reel, do you have any idea how your patient may have contracted this?"

There was a long silence. David's suspicions had suddenly been verified:

Deep under his patient's operative sites, their epidermis was undergoing an invasion. Group A beta-streptococci, introduced during surgery had started to unleash damaging enzymes and toxins that had but one purpose: To consume flesh.

David had so many thoughts at that moment, he felt as though his head was going to explode. He couldn't tell Coblentz about Dexter's death. Now though, he knew what had killed the poor ape. And now Norah Rhodes! He also knew that Cindy had left suddenly. He doubted that she would have sabotaged his work. *That only left one person.*

Finding his voice, he said, "Dr. Coblentz, you're going to have to excuse me. I need to contact someone immediately in light of all this." David pushed himself out of the big leather chair and left Coblentz standing at his desk. David could still hear him as ran to the elevator across the hall.

"Dr. Reel. We need to talk. This is highly irregul–"

The elevator doors closed and David jammed the button for the lobby.

Jean Stokes had some questions to answer.

Chapter Sixty Six

Jean Stokes pulled her car onto the road following the girl's directions. She allowed herself a rare moment of laughter when she thought of the girl, who looked as though she had fallen into a tackle box. She dismissed the thought and replaced it with a smile reserved for thoughts of fire. Jean Stokes was going to enjoy burning Olson to a crisp. He could have alerted David and ruined everything for her. Dead or not, the fact that fire was involved excited her. Just looking at the flames could almost bring her to orgasm.

She turned right and saw the sign for Pine Quarry. There, she turned onto small access road and drove another fifty yards to the entrance. She stopped the car and killed the engine. Three vultures clung to a perch along the fence. *Sentinels on a death watch.*

She took the gas can and walked up to the iron gate across the entrance. A huge metal pin, long ago rusted over, was all that held it closed. She kicked hard and the pin snapped in two with a loud metallic crack. The gate swung open and the quarry opened up directly in front of her. Piles of old tires and appliances of every kind littered the gigantic hole in the ground.

Jean Stokes turned to get Olson when a high-pitched beep broke the silence. *Had she left the ignition key engaged?* Wheeling around, she realized the sound was coming from the rear of the car–from the trunk!

Feeling her blood pressure skyrocket, she jammed the key in and it popped open.

Jean Stokes staggered backward. The stench that burst from the trunk was nothing she could have prepared herself for. The odor was so vile, Olson might as well have jumped up and hit her with the tire iron. She retched several times and gasped vehemently for breath. Finally, she regained her composure and realized the source of the sound. *Olson's pager!* Still on his belt when she'd killed him, now someone was apparently trying to reach him.

Too bad for them. In a few minutes, whoever it was would get a giant meltdown signal.

With her curiosity killing her, she put her hand over her mouth and leaned in the trunk. Olson, wrapped in clear heavy plastic, lay face down. Gagging again on the stench, she pulled him over on his side. The volume of the pager grew louder and she could see the small black device through the plastic. She pulled a layer of it back, the odor now enveloping her. Gulping fresh air from behind her, she jerked the pager from his belt. Bodily fluids ran down her arm and she cursed at the corpse. She backed up and pushed the button to illuminate the tiny screen on the device.

She did a double take to make sure she'd read it right. There was no mistake.

It was David's number at the lab! He was paging Olson.

Chapter Sixty Seven

Time was closing in on David. He left Washington General after meeting with Coblentz and roared up Connecticut Avenue toward the lab.

It was amazing him they didn't stop him for speeding. He was going at least seventy. The speed limit was forty-five. Feeling his anger boil over, he cursed himself for being so naive. He should have never hired Jean Stokes without her security check being finished. *And where the hell was Olson when he needed him?*

When he arrived at the lab, it was silent except for some scratching in the animal cages. He wanted to talk to Jean to at give her a chance to explain. However, when he stepped in his office, he realized his suspicions were right. David had a photographic memory when it came to the lab. Things weren't the way he'd left them.

Before he went any further, he bolted to the back of the lab. To his relief, the lock was still in place on the OFF LIMITS door. If anyone were to get in there, he didn't even want to think about what might happen. He was certain no one would understand the magnitude of it.

He went back to the office and looked around. The file cabinet sat partially open and several files were out of order. One file in particular stood out. And the pictures it contained were missing. David raked through the files frantically, but the photos were gone. Perplexed, he couldn't understand what Jean would want with *those* photos. He stood staring a hole in the floor when he noticed one of his answering machine tapes lying at the foot of his desk. He picked it up and stepped over to the machine. Seeing that the tape compartment was empty, he slipped the tape in and sat down.

The first couple messages were from the hospital, several days old. The next message sounded urgent. David adjusted the volume up, then replayed it. "Dr. Reel, this is Dick Olson. I need to talk with you as soon as possible regarding Jean Stokes. It appears she may not be who she claims to be. Please call me when you get this message. And by all means, keep her away from your lab."

David had tried to call Olson earlier, but the answering service had told him Olson's pager was out of order. Now, Olson's message was too late. David had possibly ruined his life's work. He struggled to keep his emotions in check. As a curtain of fatigue fell over David, he dropped into his chair and tried to review what he needed to do tonight. He couldn't believe he'd trusted Jean Stokes–or–whoever she was. And that was the question. *Who* was she?

Chapter Sixty Eight

Norah Rhodes awoke gradually from her drug induced sleep. As the seconds passed, she became more aware. Norah began monitoring her internal messages.

A big question loomed in her mind: Am I all right? Feeling rudely betrayed by her surgery, she wondered if some new catastrophe awaited her. *Could her body have rejected the graft?* That had been her main fear immediately after seeing the blotches. *Could the graft have come loose?* Tentatively, Norah sat up. There was no longer any pulling knifelike pain although her face seemed to feel numb.

Outside the hospital room, the voices of hurried doctors and nurses reverberated down the hall. The noise offered a modicum of relief to the quiet confines of her room.

Norah entertained the idea of calling a nurse, more for the opportunity to just speak with someone who might calm her fears, than for anything else.

The disagreeable numb sensation that had plagued her earlier, now became more intense and began to spread. Norah could feel it on her face like a cold liquid. The concern that something had gone wrong on the inside reasserted itself. At the same instant, she noticed a wetness on her pillow that alarmed her.

That was strange!

Feeling a sudden chill, Norah looked carefully at the top of her hospital gown. It was as saturated as a wet rag, and there was a strong, rancid odor coming off of it. Norah felt her fear begin to grow.

In slow motion, Norah got up and walked to the bathroom. It was only ten feet from the bed, but it seemed like a mile. The floor tilted underneath her, and she hugged the wall until she got to the sink and steadied herself. She looked closely in the mirror and could now see the source of the wetness. The gauze dressing covering her face was soaked through with a pink frothy drainage. The tape that held it in place was loose and the dressing came off easily. She gently peeled it back and the odor suddenly overwhelmed her. Norah gagged. Then, it all dropped into the sink.

Everything.

Lacking any facial flesh, she had no expression, but the eyes were wide. Even the delicate nose David had painstakedly sculpted for her had sloughed off.

Norah Rhodes ran toward the window and envisioned the face of The Phantom of the Opera as her own.

And it was!

* * *

The earsplitting crash sent a shock wave down the hall.

When the charge nurse heard it, she dropped the chart she held, and bolted toward the sound. She knocked over two other nurses who came into the hall when they'd heard it. Bursting into Norah Rhodes' room, she came to a screeching halt just inside the door. The nurse stared blankly.

She was a minute too late.

* * *

Asleep at his desk from sheer exhaustion, at seven a.m. that morning, David barely heard the phone ring. When he finally picked up, he was surprised at the voice on the other end.

"David, it's Paul. I think you better get to the hospital. It's one of your patients. The woman in your trial."

"Norah Rhodes? What is it Paul, what happened?"

"I can't say, David. Just get to the hospital as fast as you can."

The dial tone clicked on before David could ask him anything else. Judging by the tone of Paul's voice, David knew whatever had happened must be serious.

He didn't think it could get any worse.

Chapter Sixty Nine

When David rolled to a stop in front of Washington General Hospital, a uniformed policeman at the entrance to the main parking lot barred the way. He directed him to the staff lot, which had been opened to the public, "Until we straighten this mess out here," the officer told him. Eighty to a hundred feet behind him was a cluster of Metro D.C. cruisers and other official vehicles, some with emergency beacons rotating and flashing.

Not satisfied, David rolled his window back down. "What's going on, officer?"

"We've got this lot blocked off right now. You'll have to use the visitor lot."

"I'm a physician, here. I need to get in right away."

"I'm sorry, doctor, orders are orders."

As he followed the patrolman's directions and headed toward the staff lot, David glanced to the left and saw a crowd had formed outside the lobby. Police were doing their best to keep them behind the yellow tape. Above them, uneasy patients gazed out their windows. Aware that something was wrong, but not sure what.

By the time he slotted the BMW between two cars with MD plates and ran back to the hospital driveway, David had convinced himself that something had gone terribly awry with his patients.

He looked up and his heart sank.

On the fifth-row of windows, one was shattered. Shreds of material clung to the sharp edges. His eyes followed a straight line down the building until he caught the scene on the ground. A sheet covered *something?*

David bolted across the macadam.

Paul Gallo stopped him halfway. "Don't, David."

"Paul, please."

Paul shook his head. "I'm sorry. It's your patient. Norah Rhodes. She...she leaped to her death."

David's legs suddenly seemed to liquify. "Oh my God. How...I mean...wh...?" David collapsed on the curb, his face in his hands.

Paul looked down. "I tried to call you last night." She took a turn for the worse. The antibiotics just couldn't stop the bacteria. By this morning, the poor girl's face was nearly obliterated. I've got more bad news too."

David stared past Paul toward the pulsing emergency beacons. He saw a morgue wagon with the patrol cars.

"Vorrell wants you in his office right away," Paul said. "I covered for you David as much as I could, but you need to be here when your patients have a problem. And that's not all of—"

"I was at the lab, Paul. I was..." David didn't know what to say. Norah Rhodes was dead, and it was his fault. Just like his mother, she had taken her own life. *It wasn't fair. If he'd only stayed home that day as he'd planned. Or insisted that his mother call the doctor.*

"David...David," Paul's voice persisted.

David looked up into the broad face of Paul.

"I just got a page from the nurse on three south," Paul said. "She's hysterical." Paul swallowed hard and took a deep breath. "She changed Chip Conroy's dressing, and...his flesh came off with it. He's still unconscious thank God."

With a tightness in his chest, and a throbbing in his temples, David said, "Jesus, Paul, can this get any worse? I don't understand what went wrong."

"I don't know. You'd better get up there. I'll hold the wolves off for you."

David shook his head. "I can't help feeling that someone is deliberately sabotaging my work."

"That's a serious accusation. Who would do that?"

"Amazingly, I think I have a pretty good idea."

Chapter Seventy

Jeffery Vorrell cleared his throat several times then bore down on David. "Doctor Reel, do you have any idea what you've done to the reputation of this hospital?"

"I don't know what went wrong. I believe someone is trying to ruin me."

Vorrell rolled his eyes. "Doctor, you have a dead patient, and another one who might as well be. You are *already* ruined. FDA called this morning. They've pulled the plug on you."

David slumped forward, his whole world collapsing around him. Without the FDA behind him, they might as well banish him to another planet. He found his voice. "I need more time to find out–"

"There is no more time, Doctor Reel. If you think I'm going to believe some cockamamie story about sabotage, you can forget it. Face it, you screwed up. And because of it, people are dead. I tried to warn you. I had reservations about this whole thing from the beginning, but I wanted to believe in you. Big mistake. Now we all have to answer. You especially. As far as this hospital is concerned, your privileges here are suspended pending a thorough investigation by the FDA and Washington Hospital Group. Good day, Doctor Reel."

David stood up. "What about my patients?"

"I think we have staff here that can handle your patients in a safer manner than you apparently can."

Feeling his anger rise to the surface, David leaned down until his face was directly in front of Vorrell's.

"Let me tell you something you little insect. I have given my heart and soul to my patients. Someone tampered with my surgeries. Now whether you want to believe it or not, it's true. And I intend to prove it. And after I do I'll take my work to another hospital where they will appreciate it, and where I don't have to put up with little men like you who have a complex."

Vorrell was shaking when David finished and he cleared his throat at least ten times, which was a lot, even for him. David slammed the door and headed to the elevator. *Maybe for the last time?*

Now he would find out once and for all, who Jean Stokes really was.

Chapter Seventy One

Ghastly visions plagued David as he tore out of the hospital parking lot and down Connecticut Avenue.

Norah Rhodes' face. It wasn't the beautiful face he'd created for her. Instead, it was a horribly distorted mask of death. Pockmarked with throbbing sores that spewed forth foul green drainage. Sores that could only come from one source: *Necrotizing Fasciaitis!*

Coblentz told him it was in the cultures. Norah Rhodes was the source of those cultures. That only meant one thing. Jean Stokes must have contaminated the graft skin. But why? Jean seemed like the perfect assistant.

Perhaps too perfect.

David flew up Massachusetts Avenue toward his house. He drove faster yet, weaving with greater aggression from lane to lane, taking bigger risks to the accompaniment of blaring horns and the squeal of brakes. He almost wished a policeman would pull him over. It might help erase the vision of Norah Rhodes, lying twisted and bloody below her hospital window.

It had been too much for her to take. The promise of a new life, a new face. Extinguished before she could even enjoy it. David's guilt ate at him as it had his whole life. His mother's death had left a hole in his heart another lifetime couldn't fill. He felt compelled to make impossible decisions, commit horrific acts–acts he never imagined himself capable of.

He still had one chance to make it up to her. If he failed, he would never forgive himself. He had promised his mother, and he had promised Sam.

David needed to find Jean Stokes. That would save his reputation.

He also needed to finish what awaited him at the lab–that would save his sanity.

Or perhaps rob him of it.

Chapter Seventy Two

The sky brightened from black to gray-black as David pulled up to his townhouse complex. The homes sat on a private street in an upscale area of Bethesda. Since he purchased it two years earlier, he'd spent so much time at the lab he felt like a stranger when he did manage to get home. He looked with pride at the house, a copy of a Victorian, complete with gingerbread trim and classic Williamsburg colors. He'd hoped to one day start a family in this house. Now he realized he'd probably lose it along with everything else.

When he got to the steps, three-days worth of newspapers awaited him. He slid them under his arm while he corralled his door key. As he wrestled with the papers, his eyes diverted to the lower-left corner of the paper on top. He scanned the caption and the accompanying photo. David looked a second time, then stopped dead in his tracks.

His mouth agape, he opened his door and dropped onto the sofa without ever taking his eyes of the picture.

It was Jean Stokes!

Next to it in bold letters read:

POLICE CONTINUE SEARCH FOR SHEPARD PRATT ESCAPEE.

Had it not been for his fatigue, it would not have been so long in coming to him. As it was, the hair dye did it. He knew who she was then before he even read the article. The realization hit him like a brick on the head.

There was no Jean Stokes working for him.

The familiarity he always felt when she was around. Her eyes, the smile. Things he had indelibly buried in his childhood memories. Her current hair color was fake; the news photo, no doubt taken years before, showed her true color—red. That was the way David remembered her:

Sam's little sister, Molly.

All grown up now, and with more pathologies than most textbooks cover.

The newspaper article recalled all the sad details of Molly's life. It took a jury eighteen minutes to find Molly Cousins innocent by reason of insanity of the murder of twenty-six co-eds. The defense presented its case cut and dry: Miss Cousins lost her mother and father when she was four. They sent her, along with her older brother to live with her aunt, Lyla Cousins. A year later, that same brother, her closest blood-relative, and her role model, burned to death in a horrible fire when she was five. They treated her for depression and psychosis, but due to her high intelligence, she was able to fool her doctors into stopping her medicine in her junior year of high school.

Other students had ridiculed her all her life, and in college it just got worse. Finally, when she could take no more, she snapped. She acted out in the way she hurt the most. Her brother, the only thing she felt she had left after the death of her parents, was burned up in a fire, so she felt compelled to burn up anyone who hurt her.

It was as the defense said, "A simple case of a doctor who failed his patient." Had Molly stayed on her medication, she would have been able to cope. It wasn't her fault. The world dealt her a rotten hand.

David flipped the page and continued to read.

The case was so well presented, and so true, the prosecutors didn't even argue. They would institutionalize Molly Cousins at Shepard-Pratt Hospital for the Criminally Insane for a minimum of twenty years. Being in a facility near her home would allow her only living relative, Lyla Cousins, the same aunt who raised her, to visit.

The psysiciarist at the trial felt there was little hope of Molly ever returning to society as a normal person. Her childhood had been so traumatic, she had built a wall of anger that no therapy could penetrate. Medication could control her, but unless supervised there was no guarantee she would continue to take it. And without it, someone else was likely to become a victim.

David tossed the paper aside and bounded to the kitchen. The phone book sat on the counter and he flung it open and scanned its pages. He had no idea if Lyla Cousins was even still alive, but it was worth a try.

Surprised that he'd he found the number, suddenly memories of Sam came flooding back. The number was the same one he'd called him on every day when they were kids. David realized Lyla Cousins must be at least eighty by now, and he doubted if she'd even remember him.

Hands trembling, David dialed the number. A dull nausea swept through his gut as he dredged up old memories as fast as his mind could think. Sad memories of his best friend. He let it ring for what seemed like an hour and he was about to hang up when a frail voice answered. "Hello."

"Is this Lyla Cousins?"

"Yes, who is this?"

"My name is David Reel. I don't know if you remem—"

"Oh my God. She's come after you, hasn't she?"

Chapter Seventy Three

It started with the death of Sam, Lyla Cousins recalled to David. The happy days of her big brother walking her to school each day were gone.

Death holds no permanence for the six-year-old mind. Molly fully expected Sam to ride up on his bicycle like he'd done so many other days. Time passed though, and he never did come back. Eventually, with the help of her aunt Lyla and many counselors, Molly learned to accept that her brother was lying in the cold ground of St. Mary's Cemetery for all eternity.

Children tend to blame themselves when they lose a loved one. Molly was no different. For a long time, she faulted herself for Sam's death. Perhaps some sibling disagreement they'd had, or a name she'd called him. As years passed and Molly matured, the self blame soon turned outward and she looked for someone else to blame. Her anger festered, and by high school, she could have self-combusted as easily as if she'd had lighter fluid running through her veins.

To make matters worse, fellow students took every opportunity to remind her she was an orphan. She didn't have the latest fashions, and she didn't go to social events other students did. Her aunt tried to provide for Molly the best she could. With her limited resources though, she couldn't afford the popular things other girls had. All this led to a very depressed and *very* angry young woman.

The one bright spot in Molly's life was her intelligence. She excelled in everything academic, and eventually won a scholarship to Cal-Tech in the summer of 1991. It was a happy day for Molly when she read the acceptance letter to her aunt. She also walked to the cemetery that day to read the letter to Sam. She knew he would be proud of her. His little sister about to study molecular biology at a big university in California.

That same day, Molly made a promise to Sam. She promised to avenge his death. "It wasn't fair. David Reel caused you to die," she said to the marble grave marker.

She had found her scapegoat. Her obsession to blame someone reached it crescendo that summer. She would keep track of David Reel until she avenged Sam's death.

David listened as the heartbroken old lady described how the once sweet child she loved as her own, had become "a monster." Worst of all is what happened when Molly left for college.

When she arrived at Cal-Tech that fall, she carried a lot more baggage than what she had under her arms. With her traumatic childhood and deep emotional scars, she was on short fuse–extremely short.

She learned early to suppress her anger at the world for ripping her loved ones away from her. Therapist after therapist tried to reach Molly, but failed. Time was the only thing that would bring her anger to the surface where she could vent it. While her roommates worried about their next date, Molly stayed in her dorm to study. Socializing was uncomfortable. Soon, as in high school, she had become the brunt of many jokes. Some even accused her of being a lesbian.

The anger just beneath the surface was now to the boiling point. After a particularly cruel session of ridicule by two of her roommates, Molly decided she had taken enough.

Just after midnight on a chilly April night, she slipped out of the dorm and walked to the local 24-hour convenience store. There, she purchased a one-gallon plastic gas container and filled it. Taking it back to the dorm, after explaining to the security guard that she'd run out of gas, she poured the entire contents in a line around the dormitory. Then, with as much thought as one would give to lighting a charcoal grill, she threw a match to it.

She ran to the other side of the campus as the building went up like a tinderbox. The fire trapped twenty-six coeds inside. Before the first engine company could arrive, the girls were literally roasted alive. Most never woke up, succumbing to the carbon monoxide.

Molly ran so hard she lost her shoes, but still ran until her feet bled and she collapsed. The police found her incoherent in a vacant lot next to the convenience store where she had purchased the gas.

It wasn't hard for the police to figure out who started the fire, after the store clerk identified her as the girl who had bought the gas just twenty minutes before the blaze.

Lyla Cousins still cared deeply for Molly, she told David. But she was scared to death of her. Molly had not tried to contact her since she'd escaped Shepard-Pratt. The police were in touch with her frequently in case Molly showed up.

David sensed the desperation in the old woman's voice. Torn between her love for Molly, and fear for herself. David shared that fear. Not for himself physically, but for his reputation.

The truth was inescapable—Molly Cousins blamed David for her brother's death. And in doing so, had doomed his two trial patients, and probably killed Cindy Rudolph as well.

Now, as David listened in stunned silence, he knew what Molly wanted.

She wanted revenge.

Chapter Seventy Four

David thanked Lyla Cousins and hung up the phone. He promised her he would try to help Molly if it was still possible. David's mind was a whirlwind of emotions. Despite what Molly had become, he couldn't help feel sorry for her. He'd often wondered about her as he grew up, but after his mother took her life, David had enough of his own mountains to climb. He slipped into a deep depression, and if it weren't for Charlie and the help of several good psychiatrists, David may have ended up like his mother. Instead, he became a survivor. Molly apparently had not. After what he had learned about her, it was clear he was dealing with a psychopath. Still, David understood. His own sanity lately was fragile, at best. He managed to hide it due to his status as a doctor. But he knew the common thread than linked he and Molly: *their grief.* The crushing blow of him losing his mother and Sam. And for Molly her parents and Sam.

David was able to channel his heartbreak into his work. *Some of which the public knew, and some that it did not.* That was his secret, however, and no one but him would understand it. Except maybe Molly. Even though she was out to destroy him, she might understand his compulsion. Or would she?

Struck by a sudden stab of fear, he rushed out of his house, bounded down the front steps and clambered into his car. He needed to get to Molly and show her the truth about the fire. The whole truth.

Chapter Seventy Five

The room at the nearby Motel Six smelled musty and felt too humid. Molly Cousins sat on the bed, flicking the small butane lighter off and on, off and on, watching the flame dance for a few seconds, then letting it die. Exhausted, her last few days had taxed her to her limits, and now she'd begun to hallucinate. She thought about Jean Stokes, and how she'd used her name to fool David Reel. It hurt her to know she was doing things in Jean's name that Jean would never do. She loved Jean like the sister she never had.

Molly met her when she arrived at Cal-Tech her freshman year. A native Californian, Jean Stokes was as progressive as a teacher could be without getting in hot water with the administration. With her long flowing dark hair, tie-dyed tee shirts beneath flannel, she was the quintessential hippie professor. She was also highly intelligent, but not to the point of being an egghead. Many professors only cared about their students test scores. Jean, however, was very much in tune to her students feelings.

When she befriended Molly, Jean sensed Molly's troubles right away. An awkwardness that Molly tried to hide. She also soon realized how extremely smart Molly was. A trait they both shared. As their friendship grew, Molly confided in Jean at every level. They spent many hours in the lab discussing everything imaginable. By the end of the first year they had built a solid friendship and for the first time in Molly's life she felt secure.

At the same time though, Jean developed a nagging cough. As a heavy cigarette smoker, she was smart enough to figure out the cause. But she grossly underestimated the seriousness of it.

At Molly's urging, Jean went to the campus clinic for a checkup.

After a preliminary exam, the doctor ordered a routine chest X-ray. What came back shocked him. Jean had not only one tumor in her left lung, but a second even larger one in her right. Both were the size of grapefruits. Both were inoperable.

Tears formed in Molly's eyes as she recalled the day Jean returned home and gave her the news. Molly knew it was bad: she had never seen Jean look so depressed.

"Well, kid," she had said. "They gave me two months"

They sat and held each other, too numbed to speak. After Jean left that day, Molly's grief soon turned to anger. Enraged, she retreated to the lab and prowled the aisles. "Here we go again. Taking away someone, I love. *Here we fucking go again!*"

Then, in true Molly fashion, she picked up a Bunsen burner and incinerated every lab-rat in the animal room.

Now, trying to shake herself back to the present, Molly remembered how relieved she had felt after that. She was hoping for that same relief again.

She was in a dangerous mood. And it was only two blocks to David Reel's lab.

Chapter Seventy Six

With his future at stake, David screamed down 495 without so much as a thought about speeding. He weighed the risks, and his risks at the lab far outweighed anything the police could do for a traffic violation. It was another ten minutes to the lab. *He needed to get there in five.*

As David drove through Rockville and onto the expressway, he cursed himself.

"Why am I always so naive?" he said aloud. David slapped the steering wheel in embarrassed anger. When Molly showed up posing as Jean Stokes, her beguilement had undermined his good judgement.

Fear stuck in David's throat when he pulled into the lab complex. He felt a short-lived sense of relief when he didn't see Molly's car. Then, he remembered, she had said her apartment was within walking distance. It took every bit of self-restraint David possessed to keep from bolting to the lab door. Instead, he tapped on his steering wheel. *How could his life change so drastically in two days?* With two people dead, and his life's work in jeopardy, had it all been worth it? He wondered.

David saw movement at the window. He shot up in his seat and considered using his cell phone to call the police. *Bad idea.* He couldn't explain everything in his lab.

He shifted his position and looked at the clock on the dash. Twenty minutes had gone by. Unable to sit still for another second, David started to get out of the car. He had the door half-open and one foot on the curb when he saw someone at the window again. Only this time the blind was pulled back far enough to see in.

It was Molly!

There was no doubt about it: she was waiting for him.

David froze. As if in a dream, it took him several heartbeats before he could break the paralyzing spell Molly's appearance had caused. In full panic he pushed the car door completely open and leaped out onto the sidewalk. He dashed for the building, grasping the door, fully intending to pull it open. But he didn't. After a few seconds hesitation, he cracked the door an inch and peered within.

Darkness.

Silence.

He'd never heard such quiet in the lab. Seeing the front room empty, he stepped in a few more inches. It was pitch black inside, and totally silent. He considered his options. There weren't many. He ran his hand along the wall feeling for the light switch. He touched the steel box, felt it carefully. There were three large heavy-duty switches.

He threw them on.

One by one, the overhead lights came on.

Then, from David's periphery, there was a blur of movement—a pair of hands—holding a metal pipe.

Chapter Seventy Seven

"Dr. Reel is on indefinite leave of absence."

"What do you mean?"

"I don't know the particulars. I just know he's on LOA," the hospital switchboard operator said.

Charlie Goodman rested a huge, weathered hand on the phone receiver. He looked out the window and shook his head. He'd been trying to reach David all week. When he'd still not answered after three days, Charlie called the hospital. He tried to remain optimistic, but in the face of what they were telling him, the inability to get ahold of David was progressively more distressing. Also, Charlie had received some disturbing phone calls in the middle of the night. A woman, who wouldn't give her name, asked him questions about David. *Questions with reference to David's past.* When Charlie pressed her to identify herself, she hung up. He still owned the same rotary phone he'd had for thirty-years. No caller I.D., no way to trace the call. It left him very uneasy. He feared someone was trying to gather information to steal David's work. Charlie knew it was very secretive. David didn't reveal certain aspects to the public: not even to Charlie. David told him earlier in the week he was in the middle of important surgeries. Now suddenly he's on leave of absence. It didn't make sense.

"All right. If you hear from him, please have him call me right away," Charlie said, and hung up, his face lined with worry.

His years of fighting fires had trained his mind to be calm in the face of fear. But where David was concerned, Charlie's internal discipline didn't apply. He worried. And when he did, he had a good reason.

He grabbed his truck keys and slipped on his hat. His gut instinct had guided him in raising David, and he hadn't experienced this feeling for many years. *David was in trouble.*

Something was very wrong.

Chapter Seventy Eight

David Reel awakened tightly encased in duct tape, secured to one of his own lab chairs, arms behind his back, his heart racing, his tongue thick, and thirsting for something cold to drink. His head felt as if a spike had been driven through it. A trickle of warm fluid ran down the back of his neck. He hazarded a look over his shoulder. Someone was behind him, but his vision was too blurred to bring them into focus. He tried to speak, but the words just hung in his mouth.

David fixed his bleary vision on a fuzzy silhouette in front of him.

"Well I guess I owe you an explanation, Doctor Reel. Or should I say, Davey Reel, the boy who killed my brother."

David looked up and tried to speak, but it was as if his lips hadn't got the command from his brain.

"What's wrong, Davey, not feeling too good? I've got news for you, doctor. When I get through with you, you're going to feel a whole lot worse. I'm going to cause you the pain you caused me. You took away Sam. My only brother. The only one I had left, and you killed him! Do you know what it's like to be five-years-old and lose your best friend? The only person you had left to love. To have to go to the cemetery to visit him at Christmas. Do you have any idea how painful that is?"

The fog began to lift, and David realized it was Molly talking. She sounded far away, but some of her words sank in. David's speech was thick, but he managed to get it out.

"My mother. I lost my mother too."

Enraged, Molly Cousins hurled a rack of test tubes across the

170

room. They exploded into a thousand pieces against a stainless steel cabinet, sending shards of glass everywhere.

"Your mother smoked. She started the fire, and they blamed Sam," she screamed.

David's vision began to clear and he scanned the room. It was not a pretty scene. The lab animal's cages sat overturned at odd angles. Cats, dogs, mice and rats lay everywhere. *All dead.* Bloody froth exuding from every orifice. *Necrotizing Fasciaitis had killed them all.*

David turned in slow motion. "Sam started the fire, Molly. That's the truth."

Molly Cousins stared at David and her face went through a series of bizzare twitches as though she was a marionette whose head strings had become tangled. David thought her skull was going to crack open and some nightmarish creature would crawl out from inside her. Instead, the twitches subsided, and her face resumed a normal appearance.

"So, that's the way you want it. Fine. I had hoped you would at least tell the truth before you die, and let Sam rest in peace. I see you still blame him though for what your whore-mother did."

David struggled, helpless.

His fear overflowed into anger at Molly's remark. He tugged at the tape. It was a futile attempt. It wouldn't budge.

"Enough talk," Molly Cousins said. "It's time to pay up."

"Molly, before you do this, tell me one thing. Who is Jean Stokes?"

Molly stared blankly for a second. "She was somebody I cared about a great deal. She was my professor at Cal-Tech. She was a mentor, mother, and unlike everyone else, an empathizer. The only friend I had there. But like everyone else I care about, she died too."

"Did you kill her, Molly?"

"Of course not. I loved her. She died of cancer."

"And not long after that, you burned down your dorm." David stated more than asked.

"That's right, and those bitches deserved it."

"Molly, they were innocent girls."

She ignored David and walked to the janitor closet. She returned with a small plastic bucket. David recognized the smell immediately. Cleaning fluid. *Flammable!*

She shot a glance toward David and began to pour the liquid on the floor around him. David was shocked by the contrast of Molly's two personalities. Her blue eyes were no longer soft. Now, they looked as hard as sapphires. Her mouth was no longer sensuous; the bloodless lips formed a grim line.

"They were anything but innocent," Molly said as the fluid pooled around David's feet. "All they did was ridicule me. While they were out getting screwed, I was in my room studying. I owed it to Sam to make something of myself."

"So you killed them?"

"Like I said, they deserved it. They knew I was an orphan and took every opportunity to remind me."

"I'm an orphan too, Molly. Don't you see, we're victims of the same tragedy? You don't need to kill me. Think of Sam. I can help you."

"No one can help me, David. It's over."

"No, Molly, wait. I need to show you something."

David saw the far away look come over her once again as she picked up a Bunsen-burner from one of the lab tables.

"Molly, for God sakes…listen to me! *I need to show you something. Something no one else knows about.*"

Molly Cousins heard nothing. Without another word, she tossed the burner into the lake of cleaning fluid that now surrounded David.

Flames erupted and David felt the heat instantly. Throwing his head back, he screamed at the top of his voice. He knew it was futile, and soon smoke rose to choke him. He rattled his hands violently against the tape, and even tried to bite at it. It was an inconceivable predicament. He watched helplessly as Molly Cousins left by the front door.

In a fit of panic, David tried to lift the chair off the floor and walk with it, but he was bound too tightly. Suddenly, an idea occurred to him. It was twenty feet to the door. The fire was limited to a small ring of flames surrounding him. It was also perilously close to the oxygen concentrator he used for the growth chambers. His mind didn't even want to contemplate what would happen if the flames reached it. He slid the chair, inches at a time toward the door. It was painfully slow, but it appeared as if the fire was burning itself out. Now, he had a new problem. As the flames extinguished themselves, toxic smoke began to fill the room.

David was reliving the nightmare from his childhood all over again.

Chapter Seventy Nine

Les the crematorium attendant had a nose for smoke. It went with the territory. His company equipped their facility with the latest emission reduction equipment available. Normally the amount of smoke emitted from their furnaces was so minute it was impossible to detect. Otherwise, concerned citizens would be calling the local EPA office to complain of a horrendous odor coming from the local industrial area. *Burnt flesh tended to create such odors.* This odor, however, Les detected, did not come from his furnace, even though at the moment, there was a body in each of his two ovens. When he peeked out his door to get a better whiff, he saw the source.

Across the parking lot, smoke was bellowing out the windows of an adjacent building. He had no idea who owned it, or if anyone even occupied it, but it threatened the whole complex. Although fire was his constant companion, Les had no desire to become a victim of it. He hit the speed dialer on the telephone. *911.*

Chapter Eighty

Although Charlie Goodman was getting along in years, his mind was as sharp as ever. When the police scanner in his truck started to squawk about a fire in the Rockville Industrial Complex, he did something he rarely did since leaving the fire department: exceed the speed limit.

David's lab was in that complex! Charlie's driving skills hadn't diminished. He'd driven fire and rescue trucks for thirty-years. He was in fact, a first rate driver, with a spotless record at the age of sixty-six. His driving skill and experience didn't help him, however, when an inexperienced sixteen-year-old on a cell phone slammed into the driver side of his compact Chevy truck.

Like shiny metal teeth, the chrome front end of the oversize SUV bit deep into Charlie's door. Worse, the sheet metal between the door sheared off his legs as if they were mere butter.

Time seemed to stop. He felt pressure below, but couldn't lift his head, blood gouting out of his amputated limbs like a clogged showerhead. A heavy fog enveloped Charlie, and he could hear the familiar sound of the fire siren somewhere nearby. For the last time.

Chapter Eighty One

David Reel felt as though he was in a time warp. As he inched toward the lab-door, he saw that night back in 1978 before him all over again. This time, smoke not only filled the air, it filled his mind as well. Vivid memories of his mother's screams, glass exploding, furniture melting like candle wax. Sam jumping out the window, his body already on fire. And him, unable to help either one.

As emotion overwhelmed him, David's eyes flooded with tears. For the second time in his life, he felt certain he was going to die.

Chapter Eighty Two

Holland Carter understood the D.C. police's reluctance to help him. He had played the trump card himself a time or two. Instead of being mad, he simply took it upon himself to investigate out of his jurisdiction. He painstakedly pieced together, clue by clue, the trail of Molly Cousins. D.C. wasn't interested when he'd contacted them about a possible threat to David Reel. They were even less thrilled to have a Baltimore cop sticking his nose in. But the extent and depth of Carter's curiosity, and the great sympathy that accompanied it, forced him to admit to himself that his feelings for this girl were different from his feelings for all other criminals whom he had known in twenty years of police work. *Good thing.* His unusual involvement and empathy had led to David Reel. Carter knew about the common thread between Reel and Molly Cousins. *A fire years ago.* He also knew Cousins had killed Spence. After his informant traced Don Spence to Reel, it didn't take long to figure out the rest. *Why* she killed him, was still a mystery. And what connection Spence had to David Reel, Carter had yet to figure out.

Now, as Carter crashed through the door of Reel's lab, he knew he'd been right. He covered his mouth with his jacket as smoke poured from inside. Reel lay unconscious just feet from the door, taped to an overturned chair, his hair matted with dried blood. The lab was largely undamaged except for a black haze of smoke. The fire had fizzled out as the accelerant burned off.

Reel stirred, as if he desperately wanted to speak but as if some great force was restraining him. His stricken mouth twisted, worked, but soundlessly. He shuddered, shook his head, groaned.

Carter grabbed the top rail of the chair and drug Reel outside, just as the first fire trucks arrived.

Chapter Eighty Three

Like the last scene from the *Wizard of Oz*, David Reel awoke to find himself surrounded by a cast of characters from what he hoped was a bad dream. And although he soon realized it was no dream, the characters in the hospital room might just as well have been the Tin Man, Scarecrow, and the Cowardly Lion, for all the attention he paid.

David only had one question.

"How is my lab?"

"It's fine," Paul Gallo said. He'd stood watch over David for the last three days.

David looked across the room.

Jeffery Vorrell cleared his throat a few times, then stepped toward the bed.

"Doctor Reel, I owe you an apology. You were right about the sabotage. We found a letter from the girl. It explained everything."

David sat up. "The girl. What happened to her?"

"They don't know," Paul Gallo said. As it stands right now, she's still at large, which by the way, still puts you in danger. Do you have any idea who she was?"

"Yes, I do. But it's a long story."

"Well maybe when you feel up to it we can talk about it."

Vorrell peered down at David. "Doctor Reel, I want you to know, as soon as you are up and running again, you'll have the hospital's full cooperation to continue your trials."

David smiled, but said nothing.

Vorrell smiled back awkwardly and excused himself.

"Who pulled me out of that fire?" David asked.

"Some detective from Baltimore."

David frowned. "Detective?"

Paul Gallo nodded.

David Reel looked out the window and noticed nothing. "Paul, tell me. How badly was my lab damaged?"

"Is that all you think about, David?"

"I need to know. Was the back of my lab damaged?"

Paul Gallo heaved a sigh. "If you mean the part, you've secured like Fort Knox, no. I don't see how anything short of a nuclear bomb could damage that. I was there looking around when the Fire Marshall came. Hope you don't mind? Just professional curiosity. It was mostly smoke damage."

David sank back on his pillow. "Thank you, Paul."

He was already anxious to get back there.

Chapter Eighty Four

Three Months Later

Every tier was full at Washington General Hospital's amphitheater. David Reel gazed out from behind the curtain at the chaos of jostling reporters and medical experts. Everyone awaited him. David had arrived earlier that morning with several assistants, and set up his display behind the curtains. Today he would finally reveal the trial results of Reel Skin. He had invited the nations five largest media networks here and promised them the greatest leap ever made in the field of skin grafting.

Everyone knew what he'd been through after nearly being killed a few months earlier. The Washington Post had ran his story as a lead for several days. After his recovery in the hospital, he'd become a recluse. Charlie's death had been the final blow. In fact, no one but a few close assistants, and a detective who was tracking Molly Cousins had seen David in several months. This time around, Washington General had given him carte blanche for anything he needed. Motivated more by self- interest, than by guilt about being wrong the first time, now they wanted to make sure their hospital was the one to get the publicity. David didn't care. *After today he would be finished with them for good.*

Vorrell came to the podium and cleared his throat.

"Ladies and gentleman. As you know, we are here today to see medical history in the making. Our own Doctor David Reel has graciously agreed to share the results of his latest trials of his revolutionary lab-grown skin. It is an especially bittersweet day in light of what he has endured recently. I don't want to dwell on that, however, we are here to celebrate his success. So without further delay, I give you, Doctor David Reel."

The curtain parted and David appeared between two huge sarcophaguses that occupied a large portion of the stage. Clear plastic tubes jutted from the back of each one and snaked across the floor, then behind the curtain. From the audience vantage point, only the sides of the chambers were visible. A blue tarp covered the glass top of each sarcophagus. A faint hum emitted from them, only audible to David. The lights dimmed and a large video screen dropped down behind David. The murmuring in the audience stopped as if everyone had become mute at once. David found it slightly uncomfortable. He unbuttoned his jacket and adjusted the small microphone on his lapel.

"Ladies and gentleman. Twenty-years ago, there was a terrible fire. Some of you in the audience may remember. Some may not. I remember though. All too well. In that fire, I lost my best friend, and it burned my mother beyond recognition. She lived with her disfigurement…until she could no longer bear it. Then, one spring day, she took her life. My own life as a twelve-year-old boy, changed forever. But I swore the day I buried her…I would find a way to make it up to her. Even if it took my whole life. Today, I am happy to say, I have kept that promise. And in a far better way than I ever imagined."

David looked out at the crowd. Their expressions were somewhere between surprise and sympathy. He sensed this is not what they wanted to hear. They were interested in his product, not his life story. *They would hear anyway.*

He walked to the podium just to his right and picked up the remote slide control, then keyed the device. The first slide appeared on the screen behind him. It showed an attractive woman with long radiant black hair and a brilliant smile. After a minute, David keyed the next slide.

Gasps erupted from the crowd. It was a horrendously disfigured face, obviously from a severe burn. It was hard to distinguish male or female; the fire had obliterated all the hair. After showing the photo long enough to drive home the point, David turned back to the audience. "That was my mother, ladies and gentleman."

An eerie quiet descended over the auditorium. David went to the metal sarcophagus on his right and yanked off the blue tarp. He reached under with his left foot and pushed a small pedal. A pneumatic hiss sounded and the apparatus rotated vertical, 45 degrees and facing the audience. Screams erupted from those with the best view, who could see what was in the capsule. A woman in the first row, collapsed in the aisle.

"And this is my mother now!" David declared.

Inside the sarcophagus, David Reel's mother lay. Not as the attractive woman in the first slide. Nor was she any longer disfigured. Rather, she was more ghastly than ever. The underlying look was one of a corpse whose casket had long since been closed. *Something that occurred only under the lawns of cemeteries.* The skin was gray and yellowish green, with unthinkable substances seeping from within.

Audience members sat in stunned horror.

David ignored them, and stepped to the second sarcophagus and ripped off the tarp. Audience members fainted and a row of reporters pushed toward the exit. *"Please wait!"* David pleaded. He jammed the pedal on the second box and it rotated into position.

The remaining crowd's confusion deepened into a panic-stricken exodus.

"This was my best friend, Sam! You see ladies and gentleman. I couldn't bear to leave them the way they were. Reel Skin made them whole again! *Don't you understand?*"

David Reel's mouth dropped open when his gaze fell on Sam's body. *What? Something was wrong!* He had been restored, but he didn't look right. David wheeled around to his mother–*her too.*

It was unthinkable.

He bolted around to the back of the sarcophagus and checked the giant umbilicus that pumped oxygen out of it.

It wasn't that.

He went back to Sam. A dark blotch covered Sam's face. David's heart felt compressed. Then slowly, it dawned on him. Even in his increasingly detached state, the scientist in him reasoned out the problem. He had designed the chambers to carry away oxygen and maintain a vacuum. That would prevent bacteria from causing the bodies to decompose. He hadn't counted on this.

Anaerobic bacteria! That can live without oxygen. Molly had contaminated all the skin produced in the lab. Necrotizing Fasciaitis was now consuming the bodies.

It was more than David Reel could bear.

Silence fell over the remaining crowd.

Then, the transformation started. Small subtle changes. David watched the audience staring at him, astonished. Something was happening to him. His consciousness took on a dream like state. He heard people talking, but they seemed far away.

Time seemed to stand still for David Reel. He looked at the still-figures of his mother and Sam. *He had failed them again.* He had expected more. He needed more. To see his mother smile again. To hear Sam's hearty laugh. *Why weren't they...what had gone wrong?* Molly was right. It *was* his fault.

Chapter Eighty Five

Paul Gallo stood in a freeze frame of disbelief. He was in the audience and saw David's meltdown. Paul knew what had happened. He had seen David change before. Only this time, it was much worse.

Paul bolted to the stage and David stared at him, glassy-eyed and catatonic. It was obvious to Paul that David Reel was somewhere far away. Tears ran down David's cheeks and he mumbled incoherently.

"What went wrong? I promised her. I failed her again."

"It's not your fault. Come on, let's go home."

Paul led David from the stage. He realized now what David had been up to in his lab for all those months. His trial surgeries, his long periods of seclusion, even his regular practice was just a cover for his true work. It was unbelievable that he could have done such a thing. In his demented state, David fully expected that by restoring his mother and Sam with Reel Skin, he would somehow give them life again. That they would step out of their mechanical coffins and stand beside him on that stage. His dark obsession and overwhelming grief had consumed him. As brilliant as he was, his scientific mind was unable to overcome the tragedy that haunted him his whole life.

Paul Gallo shuddered at the thought as they loaded David into a waiting ambulance.

Chapter Eighty Six

Holland Carter closed the case folder on his desk and shook his head. He was disappointed, that he'd not been able to find Molly Cousins, and possibly save her from a final act of desperation. He'd questioned Reel several times before his breakdown and was satisfied that he had no idea where she was either. Once again he felt uncharacteristic empathy for her, even though she was evil personified. She was so deeply disturbed, she was one who *truly* couldn't be held accountable for her actions. Carter had never imagined he could feel that way.

Had Shepard-Pratt not stalled, perhaps he could have found her in time. At any rate, left alone, Shepard-Pratt was up to its ears in legal problems as a result of its cover up of Molly Cousin's escape. Between that, and its newest resident, it was front page news nearly every day.

Carter filed the folder away in the drawer marked: UNSOLVED. He slipped on his jacket and headed out the door. He had to be in court in ten minutes. The former administrator of Shepard-Pratt was due for her hearing on misconduct charges, and he wouldn't miss it for the world.

As he walked across the street to the court, Carter wondered who was the more demented of the two: Molly Cousins, with her penchant for burning people alive. That was bad enough. But Reel's obsession so twisted his mind that he would exhume his own mother and a best friend, then remodel their ruined bodies like some after-school science project. That defied belief. Now, the one burning question, with no pun intended.

Where was Molly Cousins?

Epilogue

It was a glorious Friday morning, and the sun cut a path across the California sky. The Greyhound pulled to a stop, and the roadside dust cleared. Out from the pneumatic hiss of the door stepped the last passenger, who had purchased her ticket five days earlier in Washington, D.C. She traveled light, with only a carry-on bag and a small purse. No need to bring much. She planned to start all over.

Molly Cousins slipped down the aisle to the door. She looked up and caught a glimpse of herself in the rear-view mirror before she stepped down. Her new appearance was working out nicely. She liked her long blonde hair. And as soon as a few small bruises cleared up, she'd be ready for her new Cal Tech I.D. photo.

She'd done the changes herself. After studying a few of David Reel's books and stealing some collagen injection, she'd managed to alter her mouth and nose. It wasn't her favorite look, but it would have to do till a more permanent job could be done.

Long before she'd left Washington, Molly Cousins had made provisions for her trip back to California. In her bag were the credentials for another identity, including a drivers license, social security card, and passport, if needed. Having taken Cindy Rudolph's picture off the document, she had easily replaced it with a current one of her own. Complete with her new, blond hair.

With the most recent edition of the Washington Post under her arm, she stepped out onto the curb and took a deep breath. The air felt so clean, so new. She had read the paper's headline and was disappointed that she had failed to get rid of David Reel. But she reminded herself, it wasn't over. *It would never be over as long as he was alive.* But for now she'd have to be content to be back at her old alma mater. *Besides, she still had some scores to settle here.*

That night, Molly Cousins wrote a letter to Rufus Davis and thanked him for all his help at the asylum. Next she wrote a note to Dr. David Reel, currently in the custody of Shepard Pratt. She suggested that she would be visiting David in the very near future, emphasizing how much she looked forward to it. She signed this in her new alias, *Cindy Rudolph*, then dropped it into a bright red envelope.

* * *

In his private room, David Reel stared out onto the hospital grounds of Shepard Pratt. The day was alive with light, with birds singing outside the window and white clouds drifting across the sky. The room was quiet and sterile. Decorated perhaps with a fear of germs in mind. That was the way David liked his room. The medicine they gave him controlled his obsessions nowadays, but left him catatonic with little affect. At least he was happy.

Finally.

Printed in the United States
53292LVS00002B/448-495

9 781424 131730